"Well, if it isn't the menace of the mountain," a deep, mocking voice said above her.

Jennifer's head snapped upright, her eyes wide. The tall male figure looming between the steam and the snow had the quality of a hallucination. But the voice—and his wide-shouldered height—were unmistakable. She sank an inch or two deeper into the bubbling water of the hot tub.

"I thought you'd be happier to see me," he said provocatively.

"Happier to...?" She stared up at him in bewilderment. "I don't understand."

"Well, now you won't have to wait so long. You can get right down to business."

"Tonight?" she said doubtfully. He didn't sound as though it was business he had in mind. An ominous thought struck her. "You are Travis MacKay, aren't you?"

He smiled, an unexpected flash of white in the darkness of his face. "Don't tell me you had any doubts."

Dear Reader,

Sophisticated but sensitive, savvy yet unabashedly sentimental—that's today's woman, today's romance reader—you! And Silhouette Special Editions are written expressly to reward your quest for substantial, emotionally involving love stories.

So take a leisurely stroll under the cover's lavender arch into a garden of romantic delights. Pick and choose among titles if you must—we hope you'll soon equate all six Special Editions each month with consistently gratifying romantic reading.

Watch for sparkling new stories from your Silhouette favorites—Nora Roberts, Tracy Sinclair, Ginna Gray, Lindsay McKenna, Curtiss Ann Matlock, among others—along with some exciting newcomers to Silhouette, such as Karen Keast and Patricia Coughlin. Be on the lookout, too, for the new Silhouette Classics, a distinctive collection of bestselling Special Editions and Silhouette Intimate Moments now brought back to the stands—two each month—by popular demand.

On behalf of all the authors and editors of Special Editions,
Warmest wishes,

Leslie Kazanjian
Senior Editor

DEE NORMAN
White Nights

Silhouette Special Edition

Published by Silhouette Books New York

America's Publisher of Contemporary Romance

SILHOUETTE BOOKS
300 East 42nd St., New York, N.Y. 10017

Copyright © 1987 by Dee Norman

ISBN: 0-373-09417-5

First Silhouette Books printing November 1987

America's Publisher of Contemporary Romance

Printed in the U.S.A.

DEE NORMAN

is the name of two good friends and Oregon writers who borrow from the experiences of their four daughters to create modern Silhouette heroines. One of the pair, married forty-four years, is a housewife-writer. The other, more adventurous, has combined her child-rearing with a career in journalism while accompanying her army officer husband on his assignments in the United States and abroad. The authors often use the spectacular scenery of their native state as background for their romantic novels.

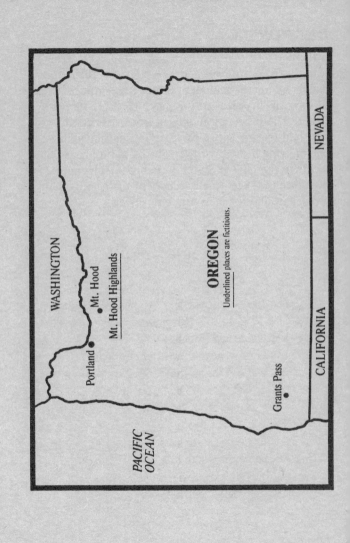

Chapter One

Jennifer Ericson stood, her ski poles firmly planted, poised at the top of Widowmaker, the experts' ski run at Mount Hood Highlands ski resort. She paused for a moment to gaze down the long white slope to the rambling old lodge that looked quaint and toy-like from this height. It had been many years since she'd stood in this spot, taking in the vista below.

The whole world around her was still. Even the faint grinding whir of the ski lift motor was lost here. The only movement she could see was in a line of empty lift chairs, swaying their way upward then down again on their continuous journey.

A faint whisper of clean mountain air caressed her face. The dark firs that marched below her up to the timberline were frosted with fresh white snow, their limbs glistening and heavy with its weight. At Jennifer's feet, the entire slope lay like a carpet spread out to welcome her. In the background, the dazzling white expanse swept up and up to where the mountain peak was etched in pure white silhouette against the deep-blue afternoon sky.

Last night's storm had blown itself out, giving way to bright afternoon sunshine and leaving an almost pristine blanket of white to greet her. The perfect landscape seemed like a good omen, Jennifer thought, that at last her heart's desire would be fulfilled. Surely nothing could snatch it away from her. Not again.

But she hadn't come up here to lose herself in the swirling midst of the hopes and dreams that had brought her back to Highlands. For now, she would think of nothing but skiing.

Jennifer thrust her poles into the deep snow and started slowly downward. She felt a thrill of satisfaction as her body responded with the old remembered skills. This very slope had once been her playground and her glory, but she had been away from it for seven long years. She was no longer the fearless teenage skier who had tackled every run headlong with visions of Olympic medals dancing in her head. Now, instead of striving for speed or form, she was just savoring the easy sweeping rhythm of lazy turns in the new snow.

One other set of tracks preceded her; Jennifer was not the only skier on the mountain. She raised her eyes to scan the slope for the other person but hastily abandoned that idea as the incline suddenly steepened and she began to pick up speed.

Now she found that she had to concentrate fiercely as she schussed straight down over short pitches, then shot out on a long traverse. She navigated an abrupt turn without difficulty and felt all the old confidence come rushing back. But the tiny moment of triumph was the prelude to her undoing as a barely hidden snag caught at her left ski. It wasn't enough to bring her down, but it shook her sure control, so that her skis no longer carved into the snow but began to sideslip. Jennifer flashed downward, traveling faster and faster. She was scrambling now, digging in her edges, trying futilely to regain command. The tips of her skis threatened to cross. Her poles flailed the air. Her balance deserted her, and she crumpled into a long, twisting, sliding fall.

She lay motionless in the snow while she drew long sobbing breaths of air into her lungs.

"Are you hurt?" The deep masculine voice came from above.

Jennifer jerked her head up in surprise, blinking snow from her lashes. The man standing over her looked immense, dark and forbidding against the sun.

"I'm all right," she said.

"Are you sure?" There was a marked lack of sympathy in his voice, almost a tinge of hostility.

Jennifer could see now that he was a striking figure, very tall, with broad shoulders, wearing a beautifully fitted ski suit of gleaming black. Of his face she could see only a hard square chin and a straight uncompromising mouth. Black mirrored goggles and a black knit cap covered the rest.

"Yes, I'm sure," she said shortly. She would have preferred to stay where she was a little longer, to catch her breath and recover her poise, but the man's uncompromising stance and unnerving black goggles prompted her to reach out for her ski poles and prepare to stand up.

He reached down, lifting her as effortlessly as if she were a child, and although she was tall for a woman, Jennifer had to tilt her head back to look into his face—only to encounter her own reflection where his eyes should have been.

"Thank you." She said it politely but without any real gratitude. His unfriendly attitude was contagious.

"You have no business being up here," he said sharply. "The lodge isn't open to the public until two days from now. And it's obvious that you shouldn't be here on Widowmaker. This is a run for experts. You'll just break your fool neck and make a lot of trouble for everyone."

Jennifer was at a disadvantage—her goggles and cap somewhere in the snow, her long dark hair tumbled in disarray around her shoulders. Her first impulse was to defend herself hotly, to inform him that this very slope had been like her own backyard for many years. That her father had been manager of the entire ski complex. That the people here remembered her and welcomed her, and of course she could ski here—whenever and wherever she pleased. And she was good, too. Probably as good as anyone he knew....

With an effort, Jennifer held back this torrent of words. She took a deep breath, then said in a deadly calm and level voice, "Everyone takes a fall now and then."

"Everyone doesn't come careening down the slope like a Chinese fire drill," he retorted. "You were all over the place. It's a wonder you made it down this far in one piece."

"And just where did you spring from, that you had such a good opportunity to come to this conclusion?"

He jerked his head to the left. "I was just coming out of the trees there, on the connecting trail. Come on, get your things together and I'll take you down."

"I don't need to be taken anywhere, thank you very much. In spite of what you've decided about my skills, I can manage perfectly well on my own. My ski just happened to hit a snag—a tree limb down on the edge of the run, I think—and I took a fall. Nothing for you to be concerned about." Even as she said the words, she wished she'd told him nothing. She wasn't required to excuse or explain herself to anyone— particularly not to this overbearing bully.

"If you're going to get stubborn about it, I'll send the ski patrol up to get you."

"Get this through your thick head. I don't need any help. I don't want any help. Just go away and leave me alone!"

He appeared to consider this. "I could take your poles away with me. Then you'd have to stay put and wait for the ski patrol."

He was big enough to do it, too, Jennifer thought. Clear hot anger coursed through her veins, making her gloved fingers tremble. She clenched her hands so he wouldn't notice them shaking and jump to another false conclusion.

"I'll make it down without any poles, if I have to," she said coldly.

He studied her for a long moment. "Well, I'm not going to carry you down," he said finally.

"Thank goodness for small mercies," she said, bending to brush the snow from her legs. "Now if you'll kindly get out of my way, I'll get back to what I was doing before you interrupted me." This sounded a little lame even to her. What she'd been doing when he arrived was sprawling in the snow, trying to get some air back into her lungs. Fortunately, he didn't take the opportunity to remind her of that.

"If you break a leg," he said, "don't bother to sue Highlands. I'll testify that your behavior was reckless and irresponsible. And that you'd been warned to stay off anything steeper than the beginners' slope."

Jennifer drew in an angry breath to reply, but he wasn't finished. "You're not bad looking," he said thoughtfully. His hidden gaze was apparently assessing her sculptured cheekbones, her smooth, tanned complexion—the face that had graced magazine covers and been the photographers' darling—and the tall, lithe body encased in the sleek sapphire-blue ski outfit that had been chosen to match her eyes. "It's a pity you're a fool."

In one fluid motion he dug in his ski poles, turned and skied away, leaving Jennifer standing there, looking after him in helpless fury.

Every fiber of her being ached with the desire to hurl herself after him—to catch and pass him and beat him at his own game. To show him who was an expert, and who belonged right here at Highlands on Widowmaker. But the distance between them was widening quickly, and Jennifer had to acknowledge the very real possibility that she might not be able to keep up with him, much less outdo him. To take another fall in his presence would be the final humiliation.

She jabbed her poles into the snow and stooped to collect her cap and goggles. Drat the man. Moodily, she brushed away the last traces of snow still clinging to her and watched his tall figure dwindle in the distance. He was a faceless, wrongheaded, bad-tempered leaper-to-conclusions. If he thought she was going to brood over his insults, he could think again. His opinion meant less than nothing to her. She would never see him again—or want to. And she knew he would drop out of her memory completely the minute she was reunited with Claude.

At the thought of Claude, Jennifer's attention shifted from her tormentor back to the lodge that slumbered at the foot of the slope. Perhaps Claude was there at this very minute. By now he could have returned from whatever errand had taken him away on this day of all days.

She had thought her heart would stop a scant two hours ago when she had walked in and asked for Claude and the pudgy boy behind the desk had replied that he was gone. For a black moment she'd thought he meant gone away, gone for good. But, no, he would be back soon—only no one knew just when. So she had wandered around the lodge, renewing old acquaintanceships, killing time. That was what she was doing here on the slope, killing time until she could be reunited with Claude. That so many years of dead time lay between the two of them didn't make these last few moments pass more quickly.

She began to ski downward again, slowly, carefully. Remembering.

Claude's image, as always, shone in her mind's eye. The fair smooth hair, the sudden smile that was white in the tan of his face. He had been a grown man when she was little more than a child. A sophisticated, charming European male. Now that so many years had passed, looking back at him was like looking into a dazzle of light, with every detail gilded by the luminous mist of long-ago love.

The charm of him, the irresistible French accent, the golden hairs on his arms. His kisses had transported her, his experienced caresses had aroused her to all the fire and sweetness of seventeen-year-old first love.

There had been just a few days of bliss, then disaster. The sudden death of her father, Nils Ericson, had triggered her mother's shattering decision to uproot the family and move them to Fort Worth near her own parents. Jennifer had stormed and wept and sworn that she would never leave, but in the end there'd been nothing else to do. She had not forgiven her mother for taking her away from Claude.

"There is nothing we can do, *chérie*," Claude had said on that final tearful day. "You must obey your mother."

She'd wanted to cry out that he could marry her, then nothing would keep them apart, but something inside her held back the words. Claude was a world-class skier who had come from Grenoble to work under her father and this was his chance to take her father's place as manager of Mount Hood Highlands Ski Area—but perhaps not if his romance with Nils Ericson's young daughter became general knowledge.

So Jennifer had gone, into seven long years of silence.

She'd made many wild plans to return: the minute she turned eighteen; the day she graduated from high school; as soon as she had a job, money, a ticket. But those days had duly arrived—and passed—and Jennifer had not left Texas. Something beyond her understanding had held her back. At first she had believed that her mother was intercepting Claude's letters. After a while she was certain of nothing. Except that she would see him again. Someday.

Now that day had finally come. Behind her lay a journey of two thousand miles. And seven years of her life.

Chapter Two

Travis MacKay strode down the central hall of the old lodge as though he owned it, something that might indeed be true in the near future if certain interested parties had their way.

He was well aware as he approached the reception desk that the trepidation on the face of the plump young clerk seated there was caused by the rumor that Travis might be his future boss. He often had that effect on underlings—especially those who were none too good at their jobs.

The clerk's reaction might be purely personal, but years of wielding financial power had taught Travis to be always alert for hidden motives. Perhaps the faint sheen of perspiration on the boy's forehead had something to do with the message he had to relay.

"I'm sorry, Mr. MacKay, but Claude hasn't come back yet. He called in a few minutes ago and I told him you were here. The forest service meeting just ended, and he'll be on his way back here as soon as possible." He said the words quickly, as though to clear himself of any responsibility for the situation.

Travis checked his Patek Philippe wristwatch and made a swift calculation. "That will take him at least an hour," he said, half to himself. "I have to pack, make a dozen phone calls and see the broker in Portland before I can leave tonight." He looked back at the clerk. "Tell Claude when he gets here that I'll see him for dinner tonight at the Benson Hotel, about seven-thirty. That will give us some time to talk business before I have to catch my plane."

"Yes, sir. The Benson Hotel, seven-thirty. I'll make sure he gets the message."

Travis started away from the desk, hesitated and turned back. "There was a young woman skiing Widowmaker," he said. "Do you know who she is?"

"A young woman—?" The desk clerk looked confused.

"Dark hair, blue eyes—"

"Blue eyes! Yes, sure." The clerk's face brightened. "Now I know who you mean. But I don't know who she is. I never saw her around here before. I do know she's a friend of Claude's."

"How do you know that?"

"She came to the desk here and asked for him. Seemed pretty upset that he wasn't here. And then she was relieved when I said he'd be back after the meeting. I don't think Claude could have been expecting her, though," he said confidentially. "Any more than he was expecting you. Not today, anyway. I mean, he didn't leave any messages or anything."

Travis looked at him coldly and the clerk's flow of gossip dried up at once. Travis turned away, unconsciously checking his watch again, the pressure of passing time fueling his impatience. Even the pleasure of his brief unexpected opportunity to ski had been tainted by the knowledge that there was so much work to be done.

A brief flash of sapphire-blue eyes intruded on his thoughts, and he tried to put it firmly aside. Perhaps he had been too rough on her. But she had been way out of control. Someone had to warn her off the dangerous slopes before she broke her pretty neck. It was true, he admitted, that he might have couched his warning a bit less savagely if he hadn't already been angry at having every single one of his appointments for the day go awry. And the Lord knew what kind of a mess would be waiting for him to straighten out when he got off the plane in Kansas City tomorrow.

A friend of Claude's, was she? Come to think of it, that was a pretty fortuitous meeting there on the slope this afternoon. Could she possibly be the competent skier she claimed to be, coming down the mountain like a runaway windmill? "Everyone takes a fall now and then," she had said in that clear low voice like music.

Everyone could take a fall, but not everyone could manage to take it right at the feet of the one man who could say yes to seventy-four million dollars' worth of development here at Highlands. Even that cretin of a clerk could tell she was Claude's good friend. Just how much was she prepared to do for her good friend Claude? Travis mused. More than once he had had delectable young women strewn in his path by someone who hoped to profit from a pending deal. Claude desperately wanted to be at the helm of an expanded Highlands, triple—or even quadruple—the size it was now. Did he want it badly enough to try setting up a little sexual persuasion to help matters along?

Travis realized dimly that he was viewing the situation through jaded emotions more suited to someone twice his age. Shrugging, he banished the whole affair from his mind, except for a small insistent voice that warned him to be on the alert and to beware of coincidences with beguiling blue eyes.

Chapter Three

The sun was low in the early November sky, and the trees threw long blue shadows across Jennifer's path as she came back to the lodge. She returned her rented skis then went to the locker room to dress for the long-awaited encounter.

She put on the clothes she had arrived in—a white tailored shirt of pure silk, beautifully fitted designer jeans that showed off the perfection of her long slim legs and fine Texas boots of burnished leather. With her height and slenderness, she could wear almost anything, from masses of ruffles to feather boas. But spare elegance had always been her signature. She traveled light. The clothes she owned were simple, but the best.

Jennifer repacked her ski things in her carryall—the kind of roomy shoulder bag that models use—then turned to her reflection in the mirror.

Intensely blue eyes, slightly tilted at the corners, gave her an exotic look. Her mass of silky hair was almost black, but it held a deep mahogany glow that added warmth and fire. Her fall in the snow hadn't affected its natural curl, and she combed it deftly into place.

Stuffing the carryall into the locker where she had left her suede jacket, she went out empty-handed to find Claude.

She was the only person in the long hallway. The faint click of her boot heels on the bare stone floor sounded unnaturally loud in the silence. The pudgy boy behind the desk looked up and eyed her appreciatively as she approached.

Jennifer asked him the same question she had asked before. "Is the manager in?"

"Yeah, Claude's back. His office is upstairs on the right." He leaned forward. "He's really busy today, but don't you worry, he's never too busy to see somebody who looks as good as you do."

He smirked expectantly, obviously waiting for her to show herself either flattered or outraged, but Jennifer looked at him with blind eyes, murmured a vague thanks and forgot him completely as she turned away.

As she walked up the stairs, the mellow old wood breathed a welcome and the shadows seemed to speak her name. Why had she stayed away so long? Here were home and happiness waiting for her to stretch out her hand.

The door to the manager's office was closed. Jennifer raised her hand to knock, but it faltered and hung motionless. After a tiny pause, it seemed to move of its own will, dropping to the knob. The door opened silently.

Claude sat at the big desk facing her, his attention on some papers in front of him, his back to the glory of the mountain that the oversized windows behind him revealed.

She stood frozen. He glanced up. The strong light from the windows dazzled her searching eyes. She could not see his face clearly enough to read his expression.

"Jennifer! *Chérie!*" He stood up and came around the desk toward her. He took both her hands in his. "You have grown up. *Mon Dieu,* you are so beautiful!"

He raised the back of her hand to his lips, bending his head slightly to brush a feather-light kiss on the smooth skin, his eyes never leaving hers. Then he deftly turned her hand over to press his lips to her palm. "Ah, Jennifer." His arms went around her. "You have come back."

She trembled in his arms. The thoughts that had seemed so clear and unshakable only moments before were all at once jumbled and incoherent. There was a small cold core of confusion inside her.

"You—you kissed my hand like that before," she heard herself say. Yes, she thought silently, and there was flickering firelight and I thought I would die of love.

"You remembered!" He sounded pleased and flattered, though somehow that wasn't the way she had meant it.

"How wonderful," he was saying in her ear. "How marvelous."

The warmth of his embrace was soothing; perhaps the world *was* wonderful and marvelous, just the way she had expected it would be.

"Oh, Claude." She closed her eyes and pressed her face into the bulky wool of his sweater. He tilted her face upward and gently, unhurriedly kissed her temple, the curve of her cheek, the corner of her mouth.

She opened all of her senses to the tidal wave of passion that she expected would break over them, engulfing them both, sweeping them both from their moorings in the mundane world—back to her dream of love.

She kissed him back.

His lips were warm on hers, but the emotion they expressed was sweet, gentle and tinged with a soft melancholy, like the long drawn-out sigh of an ebb tide.

The telephone rang, shattering the moment.

Jennifer took a step backward, profoundly shaken. She was not able to credit what her feelings were telling her. Where were the fire and the ecstasy? Had she quietly grown out of her first love sometime during the intervening years? Was that why she had found reasons to stay away for so long? Had her heart somehow known what her head did not? Her thoughts whirled in confusion and she put one hand on the desk to steady herself. She dimly heard Claude's businesslike tone as he dealt with his caller, but the sense of the words did not penetrate her consciousness. She was looking deeply into herself, and she was appalled at what she saw there.

What could she ever believe in now? Her feelings for Claude had been the bedrock of her existence for all these years. To find that those feelings were capable of dissolving like mist in the sun meant that nothing was to be depended upon. How could she trust any of her feelings ever again?

Claude put down the telephone receiver and turned back to her. "I am so sorry, *chérie*. Today I have not one minute to spare. The snows are upon us so early that in two days the lodge will be opening. So much to do—arrangements, appointments... Even to-night I am tied up, I'm afraid."

"That's all right, Claude," she said quickly, glad to be given a respite. "I really don't mind. Some other time..."

A shadow passed over his face, and she realized that her lack of disappointment had been all too apparent. His male vanity would have preferred her to be desolated at being deprived of his company. Hastily she looked away. "Everything is just the same," she said, glancing around the office, seizing the chance to change the subject. Dear familiar memories of her father were everywhere. That was his desk, his chair...

"Business has not been so good that I could elect to spend the money for new furnishings," he said defensively.

Oh, dear. Now he thought she was criticizing him for not making more progress in his years as manager.

"Many things are new," he went on, still defensively. "The chair lift, the one you see running today. All new. And the kitchen—"

"You never wrote to me." The words came out before she knew she was going to say them.

"You were so very young," he said.

"Yes, I guess I was." She turned her head away from him momentarily, toward the window. The sky had gone slate gray, and the sun was blotted out by dark clouds that were boiling up from the west. She looked back as Claude's eyes flicked quickly over the papers spread out on his desk.

Plainly torn between business and pleasure, he turned up his hands with a Gallic shrug. "On this day of all days you come back again. Please understand, Jennifer, *chérie,* it is the very future of Highlands that is in the balance today. I would not leave your side for anything less."

Jennifer realized how much she had been expecting him to drop everything and sweep her up into the center of his life. And now there was not even to be a dinner invitation. Not even a few moments to share a cup of coffee. And she was grateful. Solitude was the one thing she wanted—had to have—right now. To be alone. To be quiet. To think. Or at least try to think. To make some sense out of what had happened. Perhaps she would just sling her bag into the back of her new little Ford and keep on traveling.

She would go far away. Away from her youthful fancies—away from her own unreliable dreams. To leave would be much easier than to stay.

"I understand how busy you are, Claude." The words came out quickly, agreeably. "We'll get together some other time." She started to edge toward the door.

He looked perturbed. "Where are you staying?"

She said, "I haven't got myself settled yet—I spent last night in a motel in Grants Pass, and I still have to find a room for tonight. I suppose that Government Camp is still the nearest place to find a bed."

"Yes, we are strictly a day lodge still. But maybe not for long—" He seemed about to say more but stopped short. "I will see you tomorrow? How about breakfast?"

"I can't promise to be here for breakfast," she said, with a calm she didn't really feel. "Why don't I call you?"

Jennifer turned to walk out. Casting a look over his shoulder at the work on his desk, he followed her.

"Any other day, *chérie*—" he said as they descended the stairs.

"I understand."

She walked a little faster. He frowned. He tried to talk in general terms about the lodge and the people, but she did not respond. They collected her things, and he carried her oversize bag as they walked out of the lodge and toward the parking lot.

"Tomorrow I will snatch an hour away from the work and we will ski—"

She could tell from his voice that it cost him an effort to make the promise to tear himself away from business. Her own emotions were too agitated for conversation, so she walked beside him in silence. She felt a desperate need to be by herself, to have time to think and try to understand what was happening. To discover what had become of her long-cherished vision of love.

They reached the parking lot, vast and gloomy in the dusk. It would be jammed with cars when the season opened, but now it was nearly empty. Jennifer's compact car showed up white and solitary, well apart from the handful of other vehicles clustered near the lodge.

A thin layer of snow, left behind after the snowplow had cleared the lot earlier in the day, had melted in the noonday sun. Now that the sun was down, the frigid air had turned the small patches of standing water into treacherous black ice.

Just as they were about to step off the sidewalk, a lipstick-red Porsche turned off the highway and came through the gates. Jennifer and Claude stopped and stood watching as the driver steered toward them with headlights blazing and horn tooting. They saw the back of the car weave slightly.

When the Porsche was almost upon them, the driver braked suddenly. Out of control, the powerful car spun around, too fast for the eye to follow. When it straightened out, it was traveling backward, heading straight for Jennifer's Ford.

With a screeching crash, the rear bumper of the sports car punched into the driver's door and left rear fender of the Ford, crumpling them like paper.

The stunned silence that followed was broken only by the tinny sound of bits of metal, plastic and glass raining down on the pavement below.

After a second of shocked immobility, Jennifer and Claude ran forward.

The driver's door opened from the inside before they could reach it, and a small curly-headed blonde popped out, talking breathlessly.

"It's okay—don't worry—I'm all right!" She spread her arms and turned in a circle as though to prove that her arms and legs were still working.

"Oh, wow, what a mess!" she went on. "But I'm all right! I had my seat belt on. And it wasn't my fault, it was the ice. Wasn't it, Claude? You will tell Trav that I had my seat belt on and it wasn't my fault, won't you?"

"Are you sure you're not hurt?" Jennifer's voice was strained.

The smaller girl turned her head back and forth experimentally. "I'm just fine! No whiplash or anything. That proves it wasn't my fault, don't you think? I couldn't have been going too awfully fast if I didn't get hurt even a little bit. It was all because of the ice. So you don't have to look so worried," she told Jennifer kindly.

There was a long loaded pause while Jennifer and Claude regarded her in silence. She looked around wildly as the truth of the situation dawned on her.

"You mean—it was your car?" She struck the side of her head lightly with the palm of her hand. "Oh, hey, I'm sorry! But you don't have to worry, Trav will get it fixed up just like new. Or he can get you a new one, if you'd rather. Won't he, Claude?"

"I expect he will take care of everything," Claude said carefully. "But he may not be very pleased about this, Darla."

Her face fell. "And you're going to be seeing him tonight, aren't you? Before his plane leaves. Oh, dear, please don't say a word to him about this, will you? It will be so much better if you let me be the first one to tell him. When he's in a good mood."

"I do need my car," Jennifer pointed out quietly, trying to hang on to her composure in the face of calamity. "It's the only transportation I have, and I can't drive it the way it is."

Darla peered at the crumpled wreck through the growing dusk. "No, of course you can't. The wheels are probably all bent, or something."

"She's right, Jennifer," Claude said. "I'll be driving into Portland in about an hour. You must come with me. On the way down, I will take you to one of the motels in Government Camp, and you can stay there overnight."

"No, that won't do at all," Darla said decisively. "It's bad enough to wreck your car, we can't just park you someplace until Trav gets back. I don't know if he'll be gone one day or two. You never know with him. It might be even longer. I know—you can come home with me. Claude will call the garage and get them started on your car. Even if they can't fix it, Trav will take care of everything the minute he comes back. Will that be all right?"

The sudden change in her situation—from being able to go anywhere in the world to being stuck in this one place and not able to get out—was like a physical blow. Jennifer wanted to clutch her head to still her whirling thoughts.

"I don't know what else I can do," she said. "For tonight, anyway." She touched the crumpled hood of her car to convince herself that the disaster had really happened. In other circumstances, she could imagine that she might almost have welcomed being stranded here like this, right at the center of Claude's life. But now that her cherished romantic vision had just gone up in smoke, it was desperately important to her that she be independent. She had to be able to come and go—especially go—whenever she wanted.

She raised her head. "I'll stay with you until morning," she said to Darla. "Tomorrow I'll arrange for a rental car. And a motel."

"If that's what you want," said Darla. "Or maybe you would like to drive my Porsche. If it still runs, I mean. Can you check it and see if it's okay, Claude?"

Claude slid into the red sports car. The motor roared into instant life under his hands, and he eased it forward tentatively then drove slowly around the perimeter of the parking lot.

Jennifer realized that no one had even mentioned calling the police. Everyone expected her to take this on blind faith, trusting their assurances that the absent Trav person was going to be both able and willing to set everything right—even to the point of shelling out for a brand-new car if the old one proved unfixable.

As she stood there, motionless, she could feel the cold air striking through her leather jacket. She shivered with a combination of cold and nerves. She turned to Darla. "Are you quite sure that you can cajole your husband into paying for all this?"

"Trav's my brother, not my husband." Darla stuffed her hands into the pockets of her tan gabardine jacket. The big wooden buttons on the front were unfastened, and the casual topper hung open far enough for Jennifer to see that it was lined with mink. So brother Trav probably had plenty of money. Whether he would easily part with it was another question.

"Oh, Trav isn't usually a grouch," Darla went on, as though she had read Jennifer's thoughts. "It's just that he was in a really foul mood when he came back to the house a little while ago—even before he started packing his suitcase for this plane trip tonight. I don't know what made him lose his temper."

Jennifer shook her head doubtfully. "I hope he's not going to lose it again if he comes home and finds me there with you."

"Don't worry about that. He'll be delighted. He absolutely hates me to stay in the place alone. There's just one thing—promise to let me be the one to tell him what happened here. It will be a whole lot better that way."

"So you do expect trouble?"

"No. Really, I don't. It's just that I know how to handle Trav better than anybody. Promise you won't say a word until I have my chance. Please?"

"All right," Jennifer agreed reluctantly. "I promise."

Claude stopped the Porsche in front of the two girls. "I can't find anything wrong with it," he said.

"Oh, good," said Darla. "Just throw Jennifer's things in the back and I'll take her home with me."

"Not so fast." Claude climbed out slowly, obviously unhappy with the suggestion. "First, I believe that formal introductions are in order. Jennifer Ericson, this is Darla MacKay. Perhaps you have heard of Darla's brother, Travis MacKay, the financier."

Jennifer shook her head. "I don't know the name. But I take it that you can vouch for him."

"Of course he can," Darla interrupted. "And we're all going to freeze, standing around here like this. Why don't you just give Claude your keys, so he can have someone move your things into the Porsche?"

For the first time, Jennifer realized that half a dozen of the lodge employees had silently gathered around, called from whatever they had been doing by the sound of the crash. Obediently, she held out her key ring, and a stranger took it from her icy fingers. "My overnight bag is in the back seat," she said, "and there's a big suitcase and three cameras in the trunk."

Claude turned to speak to another shadowy figure. "Get the station wagon, Gerry. You can drive the two of them down to the MacKay house and then come back here. When the garageman gets here in the morning, I'll have him take the Porsche in, too. So he can check it over."

"Oh, Claude, stop fussing," said Darla. "You said yourself that there's nothing wrong with it."

"Nothing that I could find," he corrected her. "On level ground at slow speed it seems to handle well. But I have no intention of letting you take it out on a mountain road until a mechanic pronounces it safe."

"Well, I'm not going to let my darling baby sit out here in the cold dark all night!" Darla said fiercely.

For a moment Jennifer thought that Claude was about to lay down the law and tell her to do as he said, but when he spoke again it was to offer a compromise. "Very well, I'll have one of the men drive it down to the house for you. But only on the understanding that you agree not to drive it yourself until it has been examined. Will you do that?"

Darla hesitated. The station wagon drew up in front of them, its headlights brightly illuminating the scene. Jennifer reached out and put her hand on the other girl's arm, encouraging her to agree. Darla nodded reluctantly and climbed in.

Claude turned to Jennifer. "Are you sure you wouldn't rather drive down to Government Camp with me? I might be able to see you later."

The last thing she wanted was to be alone with Claude right now. Or later.

Hastily she got in beside Darla. "My things!" she called out as the driver put the car in gear. Another stranger opened the rear door and her overnight bag was thrust inside.

"Looks like the trunk's jammed," said one of the group around the wreck of her Ford.

"Don't worry," said Claude. "We'll get it open. And the rest of your belongings will be in the Porsche when the driver brings it down." He closed the door beside her. "Until tomorrow, *chérie*."

The station wagon started off with a lurch, and Jennifer was spared the necessity of a reply.

Chapter Four

The lights of the Porsche caught up to them just as they turned off the highway onto the long winding private road that led up to the house. After thanking the drivers of both cars, Jennifer and Darla waved as the station wagon drove away. The garage doors closed with the Porsche inside, and Darla led the way into the big chalet-style house. Jennifer carried in her overnight bag.

"How do you like the decor?" Darla said as she switched on the lights. "Trav's latest ex did a pretty good job, don't you think?"

"His latest what? Ex-wife?"

"No, Trav's never been caught, not yet. He says he's too fast on his feet for them. I meant his ex-girlfriend. When one of them starts getting too serious, I think he just looks around for a house to buy and asks her to decorate it. While she's busy doing that—nesting, he calls it—he quietly tiptoes away. To Bangkok or Buenos Aires or someplace."

Jennifer suspected that she was going to hear more about brother Trav's life and times than she cared to know, but looking around her she agreed that it was a very pleasant room.

Huge triple-glazed windows soared to the peak of the roof, embracing the outdoors while keeping the cold at bay. Jennifer supposed that the view would be spectacular in the daytime. Tonight the room was dominated by the long stone fireplace that partitioned the lower floor. Before it there were comfortable groupings of deep armchairs and sofas in warm shades of brown and amber. It seemed a little unadventurous, to Jennifer's color-wise eye, but attractive enough in a subdued way.

Darla went to the hearth to build up the dying fire. "How do you feel?" she asked Jennifer.

"How do I feel?" Jennifer sank down on the end of the nearest sofa to consider the question. "Breathless, I guess. So many things happened so fast. I feel like the world rolled over the top of me."

Darla looked back over her shoulder and nodded in sympathy.

Jennifer thought ruefully that Darla didn't even know the half of it. To Jennifer, it seemed as though her entire existence had been broken cleanly right in two—one part consisting of her whole life until this afternoon, the other of the few hours that had passed since she lay gasping in the snow, trying to draw some air into her lungs. And it seemed as though she hadn't had one full, peaceful, satisfying breath since that moment.

And she wasn't even going to have a chance to sort things out now because Darla was still looking at her. "Did you ski today?" she asked.

Jennifer nodded.

"First time this year?"

Jennifer nodded again, a little warily this time. The other girl was leading up to something.

"So you might be kind of stiff tomorrow," Darla said.

"I wouldn't be surprised. I've kept in shape, but skiing uses muscles that nothing else does."

"You don't need to worry," Darla said triumphantly. "You're going to feel just fine. Because I'm going to go out and heat up the hot tub for us."

For politeness' sake, Jennifer started to say Darla shouldn't bother to go to all that trouble, but then she held her tongue. After all, she'd just had her car smashed, all her plans upset and had been practically hijacked out here to this castle in the woods. She could use a little bit of pampering.

"My bikini's in the big suitcase. I'll have to get it out of the Porsche."

"Oh, you don't have to go to all that trouble; there's nobody here but just us girls." Darla stood up. "I'll turn on the heater. Be back in a sec."

Jennifer slipped off her jacket and leaned back into the softness of the couch, hoping that the warmth of the room and the firelight would make her drowsy and soothe away the tensions that gripped her so unrelentingly. The knot in her chest she recognized as one of the symptoms of shock, not surprising after the many shocks she'd had today.

Darla came back around the end of the fireplace carrying a wineglass half full of dark-red liquid. "You look a little white," she told Jennifer. "I thought you needed something to warm you up, so I found this wine in the kitchen. Trav probably has something stronger in the bar there, if you'd prefer."

"This will be fine." Jennifer sipped the wine gratefully. It did seem to warm that persistent cold core deep inside her.

"I bet you haven't had any dinner, either," said Darla. "Neither have I." She slapped her forehead with her palm. "And I was supposed to pick up some fresh stuff at the grocery store when I was out! We didn't get here until after noon, and right away Trav got this call to fly back to Kansas City, and Claude had these arrangements to make this afternoon, so he and Trav just have an hour or two right now before Trav's plane will be leaving. I haven't even looked in the kitchen, but I bet there's no milk or bread or anything. Let's see if we can find anything to eat.''

There were no walls to separate the various sections of the ground floor. The living room flowed first of all into the dining area at the end of the room and from there into the kitchen, which contained a smaller raised fireplace and a long polished ledge to sit on. The countertop was a terra-cotta color, and the appliances were tinted pale apricot. The table was well-waxed maple and copper-bottomed pans hung from the wall.

Darla's fears were well-founded—there was no bread or milk—and no fresh meat, vegetables or fruit.

"Oh, disaster!" said Darla. "We'll starve! Unless there's something left in the freezer from last spring."

The freezer was a six-foot-wide apricot monster that opened up to offer a moderate amount of frozen packaged food and a great deal of empty shelf space.

"TV dinners!" Darla pounced. "Lasagna." She held up the package. "How did that get in there? And I don't remember any of this other stuff. We never left it here. It must have been that oil man Trav lent the place to in August. Let's see—turkey dinner, chow mein... Why don't I just throw half a dozen of these into the microwave and we can eat whatever tastes best?"

"One turkey dinner will be plenty for me," said Jennifer. She wasn't even sure she could eat that.

"There'll be plenty to eat," Darla said happily. "And we'll have some of the wine. It'll be a regular dinner." She rummaged through the frozen packages once more and backed out holding up another in triumph. "And a cheesecake for dessert."

Jennifer laughed. "Not for me. I've been conditioned to believe that cheesecake is sinful." She took another sip of wine and felt the knot inside her slacken the least little bit. If anyone could get her to relax this night, it would be Darla.

Darla looked at her enviously. "I thought so. When I first saw you, I said to myself that I bet you were a model or something. I wish I had that kind of willpower. The way I'm going, I'll have baby fat when I'm ninety."

Jennifer smiled. "I'd say you were just nicely rounded."

"If you're rich, you're practically obliged to be thin." Darla sighed as she decided on the hamburger platter and the lasagna. "If I was just six inches taller, I'd be fine." Her eyes strayed to Jennifer's elegantly booted legs. "Like you." Darla looked down at her own well-defined curves with a trace of a frown. "You'd never know that I was a puny little thing when I was small. Travis used to call me Big Eyes, because he said there was nothing there but a little skin and bone and two great big eyes."

"You live here with your brother now?" asked Jennifer.

"Well, we don't exactly *live* here. We *stay* here. Whenever Travis can touch down for more than two minutes at a time, that is."

Jennifer was puzzled. "What about your parents?"

"A car accident—when I was nine." A shadow passed over Darla's face but quickly lifted, and Jennifer saw that it was a remembered sorrow, not a present one. "And it wasn't their fault, either," Darla added in her normal lilting voice.

"Don't you have any other relatives?"

"Just one—an older sister of Mother's. A *much* older sister. She had no husband, no kids. Not even cats. Her only passion was bridge. Did you know that you can take deluxe cruises all over the world and never do one single thing but play in bridge tournaments in the ship's salon? Even boarding school was an improvement over Aunt Mae. Travis always did what he could, but he was just really getting his career in high gear then—with his first mergers or takeovers or whatever. He was a boy wonder, you know," she added seriously.

"The schools were Trav's idea. Even though I hated every one, they at least had other kids in them. But it seems like I've spent half my life waving goodbye to Trav from the steps of some fancy new boarding school he's dug up for me." She demonstrated by assuming a forlorn expression and putting up her hand in a pathetic little half wave. Then she added briskly, "Thank goodness, those days are over. Believe me, from Switzerland to Santa Barbara, boarding schools are the pits." She looked around the warm, cheerful kitchen. "This is a hundred percent better."

Now it was Jennifer's turn to frown. Darla didn't seem to realize that she had been abandoned yet another time—that this high-powered brother had contrived to be gone once again.

They ate their dinners out of the plastic trays they'd come in and drank the wine out of fine crystal goblets.

"This is really roughing it," said Darla.

Jennifer gave her a quick glance and saw that she was serious. "Who usually does the cooking around here?'' she said. ''Whenever you have some food to cook, that is. You?''

''Nobody would want to eat anything I ever cooked. Especially not Trav. He's so fussy you wouldn't believe it. I did think maybe I'd go to *Cordon-Bleu* in Paris next year and learn a few specialties or something. But we usually get someone in to cook and run the house for us wherever we go. Claude found a girl to do it for us when we were here for three weeks last spring. She was a part-time ski instructor.'' She paused and looked at Jennifer. ''I don't suppose that you—'' She shook her head. ''No, you don't look anything like any cook we ever had.''

Jennifer smiled again. ''Well, I do know how to cook some things. But I never considered doing it for a living.'' She had been eating mechanically, listening to Darla's chatter. Now she realized to her surprise that the plastic dish was empty.

Darla went on, ''When Trav arranged to come back here this week, he thought there would be plenty of time for him to confer with Claude and to come to a final decision about whether he's going to invest in Highlands. He didn't expect all this early snow and the season opening ahead of time. I bet old Claude just about had a cow when he had to put Trav off until this evening—and then Trav had to get called away. They'll just about have time to eat their dinner before Trav catches his plane." She frowned thoughtfully. "But if we're going to be here for days and days, you and I and Trav—well, I'd better call Claude in the morning and have him start looking for someone to come in and take care of us."

"I'm not planning to stay here for days and days," Jennifer said a little sharply.

"Well, a couple of days. Until Trav gets back. That long at least." Darla's voice had a note of pleading in it. "I wouldn't want to stay in this big old barn all by myself."

"I'd hardly call this a barn," Jennifer replied.

Darla glanced around the spacious kitchen and up at the high ceiling. "Well, it is big. And it can get pretty lonesome."

"I'm not making any promises," Jennifer said firmly. She wished she hadn't been quite so eager to get away from Claude. If she hadn't accepted Darla's invitation, by now she could have been alone in the privacy of a motel room, not making an effort to be a polite guest in someone else's house. Though Darla was likable, there was certainly nothing restful about her company. "We'll see what the morning brings."

Darla's face fell. "It's because I forgot to go to the store, isn't it? Naturally you don't want to stay where you can't get a decent meal. And not even toast for breakfast—"

"Breakfast toast has nothing to do with it. I just need a place of my own. Because...because there are some things I have to do."

"But you can do anything here that you want to." Darla perked up again. "Come and see the guest room. Maybe you'll like it enough to stay."

Jennifer set her overnight case down beside a king-size bed with a patchwork velvet bedspread in creamy shades of coral and brown. Heavy matching draperies hung at the wide window, no doubt framing a marvelous view, but the night was too black to tell. The glass only reflected back the lighted interior of the luxurious room.

"I'm right next door, and Trav is across the hall," said Darla. "Come into his room, there's something I want to show you."

Jennifer started to protest, but Darla bounced out without listening. Jennifer followed reluctantly as far as the open door of the master bedroom. It looked comfortable, masculine, dull and unlived-in. The only object on the otherwise bare dresser was a small sketchbook. Darla made a beeline for this and brought it triumphantly back to Jennifer.

"Here's some of Trav's doodles. He does these on planes—whenever he has time to kill."

Jennifer leafed through the pages. They were quick sketches, faces of people she didn't recognize, done in bold slashing strokes that endowed them with personality—and left little doubt as to the artist's opinion of his subjects.

"These are really very good," she said. "Hardly what I'd call doodles."

Darla wasn't interested in the quality of the work. "Keep turning—just a couple more. There! What do you think?"

Jennifer was looking at a pencil portrait of Darla, done with more care than the others. Instead of emphasizing Darla's brash energy, the sketch showed her as a dewy, wide-eyed young innocent. Jennifer realized she was seeing Darla through her brother's eyes. "It makes you look about fifteen," she said slowly.

"But it looks just like me, doesn't it? I mean, you can tell it's me right away, can't you? I wanted him to have it framed, but he just says he'll get a real artist to do me someday."

"He shouldn't be so modest," said Jennifer. "These show real talent." Perhaps the absent Travis was a dull and stuffy businessman who would have been livelier and happier as a struggling artist.

"I think he's good, too." Darla took another long look at her picture before she closed the sketchbook and put it back where it had been. "Come on, let's jump into the hot tub."

* * *

Jennifer undressed, all of her movements slow and deliberate. Everything is such an effort, she thought. Her arms and legs felt heavy, weighted down. Maybe Darla was right, and a soak in the MacKay hot tub was what she needed.

She slid her bare arms into her lightweight ivory wool traveling robe and belted it around her slim waist as she slid her feet into quilted scuffs. Deftly she gathered up her silky mass of hair, twisted it into a coil and pinned it on top of her head.

When she came back to this room, it would be to a solitary refuge. She would be able to close the door behind her and shut out the world. She could hang on to her ragged emotions until then.

Darla was waiting for her in the hall, wearing woolly slippers and a heavy white terry cloth bathrobe. She led the way down the stairs and through the back door onto the deck.

The outside air had a sharp cold tang of fir trees and snow. Indirect lighting at floor level cast a soft, diffuse glow across the thick redwood planking. Beyond the railing, the hillside fell away in front of them giving Jennifer the odd sensation that they were suspended in space. An army of dark firs, looming ghostlike under their mantle of white, seemed to press in on either side.

The sunken hot tub was in a protected corner, sheltered from the prevailing winds but open to the sky. Lazy coils of steam rose into the night.

"I guess we don't need the underwater lighting," Darla said. She paused by a panel of switches on the outside of the house and pressed one. The water in the tub began to swirl, and a froth of bubbles appeared on its surface.

Dropping her bathrobe on a wooden bench beside the hot tub, Darla slid out of her slippers, stepped quickly into the steaming water and sat down.

After a moment's hesitation, Jennifer unfastened her robe and followed suit. The water was stinging hot as she stepped into it, but in the next breath it felt only deliciously warm and comfortable. She lowered herself onto the seat opposite Darla and leaned back against the headrest.

"I wish it hadn't clouded over," Darla commented. "On a moonlit night it's gorgeous. And there's a terrific view to the south from right here. That's one of the reasons Trav bought the place."

Jennifer stretched luxuriously. "Scenery means a lot to Trav, does it?"

"Oh, sure. And of course he says that it wouldn't be such a good investment without a view."

Jennifer closed her eyes and gave herself over to the gentle massaging action of the hot water. Darla's brother sounded like a money-grubbing old stick.

"You really are a model, aren't you?" There was a tinge of envy in Darla's voice.

Jennifer stretched again, sighing a little in contentment. "Not anymore," she said.

"Oh, that's too bad. Were you on magazine covers? Should I have seen you? I bet I have. If I just weren't so short, I'd love to be a model. Those great clothes—and all that travel . . ."

Jennifer smiled slightly at the younger girl's enthusiasm. "It sounded to me like you travel around quite a bit as it is." She slid down a little lower to let the swirling water cover her shoulders.

"But it isn't the same!" Darla protested. "And I don't get to be in magazines so everybody can see me."

"Perhaps you'd rather be in the movies," said Jennifer, humoring her. "You don't have to be tall for that."

"I don't know. Acting looks kind of hard. If I was an actress I'd want to be a good one, not just parade around like a Barbie doll or something. But I'm sure I could stand up under some lights and let them take photographs of me. And then I could be rich and famous, and wherever I'd go, people would say 'Look, there's Darla MacKay! She's on the cover of *Cosmo* this month!' Darla waved graciously to an imaginary crowd of fans.

Jennifer wondered if she had ever been quite that young and optimistic herself. "Just remember that the lights get hot and your feet get sore and you're hungry all the time."

"Oh, I'd expect to suffer a *little*. But it would be worth it. Don't you agree?"

Jennifer looked back across the years to herself at eighteen. "It *was* nice," she admitted. "For a while, anyway. But I guess my heart wasn't really in it. Modeling wasn't what I originally set out to do...."

"But you were in the right place at the right time and this dashing photographer discovered you and whisked you away to stardom before you knew it!" Darla finished for her triumphantly.

Jennifer had to smile again. "Well, not exactly, but something like that. I'm afraid that Brian isn't what you would call dashing. But he was nice. He taught me what I needed to know about modeling. And he understood why I got bored with it after a couple of years."

"Bored!" Darla's eyes were saucer-round.

"It really *is* like being a Barbie doll, you know. Some girls thrive on it, but I was one of the ungrateful ones. I felt like I wasn't *doing* anything. And sometimes I thought I knew better than the photographer. Not Brian, but some of the others—"

"Was this Brian in love with you?" Darla interrupted.

Jennifer looked at her.

"Did he want to marry you?"

After a moment's hesitation, Jennifer nodded reluctantly. "Yes, he did. But—"

"But you wanted fame and fortune and to be your own person," Darla finished up for her.

Jennifer closed her eyes again. "But at the time I believed that I was in love with someone else." The words sounded quite ridiculous to her now. What did *she* know of love? What had she ever known?

"So you're not carrying a torch for him now?" Darla's voice broke into her thoughts.

"For Brian? No, he's just a good friend. He's the one who told me that if I felt I could arrange the lighting or frame a picture better than some of the professionals, then I had better get down to business and learn the craft properly. So I did," she finished abruptly, remembering some of the hard work that had gone into attaining her present level of expertise.

"So now you're a photographer." Darla's enthusiasm was slightly dampened, but not for long. "Portraits by Jennifer," she mused. "Rock stars. Actors. The president's wife. Or do you do arty things with lots of dramatic shadows in them? Or real old people with wrinkled faces to show they have character?"

"I'm afraid I'm a disappointment to you there, too. Most of my good work has been outdoors...landscapes..."

"You mean trees and stuff?" Even politeness could not disguise Darla's lack of interest.

"Among other things. Seascapes. Deserts. Travel layouts. Animals. Wild animals can be a real challenge."

"You mean like lions?"

Trust Darla to go straight for the drama, whether it existed or not. "Well," Jennifer said, "I have photographed them once or twice. But lions are sleepy things. They *look* impressive, so big and tawny. But I prefer a livelier animal. One with a gleam in its eye."

"Like Claude?"

Jennifer opened her eyes, startled. "Whatever made you think of him?"

"Tawny animals, I guess. And old Claude's eye has a perpetual gleam in it. The Hand-kisser of Mount Hood Highlands." Darla giggled. "Has he kissed your hand yet?" She didn't wait for an answer. "He's got this technique, you see. He kisses the back of your hand—very French—and then he kisses your palm while he looks soulfully into your eyes. That's what the girls at the lodge told me."

"Does he kiss your hand like that?" Jennifer kept her voice very level.

"I think he's thinking about it. He hasn't made up his mind whether romancing me would help or hinder his chances of getting Trav to put up the money for the new lodge. He wouldn't want to get Trav mad."

"What will you do—if Claude does decide to kiss your hand?"

Darla looked up into the steam. "Oh, it might be nice to run into someone with a little technique for a change. As long as you know that's what it is. Trav always says to remember that a Frenchman can kiss your hand like crazy, but he's probably got one eye on his wristwatch while he's doing it. Anyway, Claude's awfully old. Fifty, at least."

"Not really," said Jennifer. "He's not quite forty. And well-preserved for his age," she added, with an attempt at lightheartedness.

"Really? How did you find that out?"

"My father used to be the manager at Highlands. Claude came here as his assistant years ago. I grew up not many miles from this spot."

Darla was intrigued and asked questions until she had the whole story—except for the carefully omitted details of Jennifer's infatuation with Claude. In her own mind she was already calling it an infatuation. Nonetheless, at the first opportunity, Jennifer changed the subject to skiing in general.

"What I like," said Darla, "is a whole mountain-side of new snow—and nobody's been on it ahead of me. Not a single set of tracks: that's my idea of heavenly skiing. Trav took me to Canada last year—where the helicopter flies you up this untouched mountain and you can ski all the way down with the whole slope to yourself. Once you've been helicopter skiing, it ruins you for any other kind."

"It does sound very enticing," Jennifer observed.

"There's nothing around here that can come close to it. Except—" Darla lowered her voice as though to keep the secret from the snow-laden trees that stood sentinel around them. "Since you grew up around here, I bet you know Three Mile Canyon."

Jennifer frowned. "Yes, I remember it. That's bad avalanche country."

"Well, that's the place to head after a fresh snow. It's like having your own private ski resort."

"But nobody is allowed to ski there. It's terribly dangerous."

"Not anymore. Most people don't know about it, but Claude has started having the ski patrol ski along the top and throw dynamite or something down inside. That touches off all the avalanches and makes it safe. I don't go in unless the bad spots are taken care of. And I don't go in even then if everyone and his brother get there ahead of me and track it all up."

Darla stretched and gazed around her. "Look, it's starting to snow. Isn't it pretty! You know what we need—a nice cold drink. I think I saw some cans of Coke in the cupboard."

She bounced up out of the water without waiting for an answer, exclaiming dramatically as the frigid air hit her wet skin. Snatching up her terry cloth robe, she flung it hastily around her.

Jennifer's lighter robe was caught up with the other. It floated lightly through the air and landed, sleeves first, half its length in the steaming water.

Jennifer started forward to rescue it. Too late, she pushed the sopping wool back onto the redwood deck.

"Oh, dear," said Darla. "I hope it isn't ruined." She picked up the dripping garment. "I'll go hang it up inside. And I'll find you something else to wear."

"Just bring me anything," said Jennifer. "A big towel will do." She raised her voice after Darla's retreating back. "A towel will be just fine!"

Chapter Five

As Travis MacKay pushed open the heavy front door, a sudden gust of wind caught it and slammed it back against the wall. He swore softly as he elbowed it shut. With his suitcase in one hand and bulging briefcase in the other he surveyed the brightly lit but empty rooms.

"Darla!" he called. There was no answer. He advanced to the foot of the stairs and called again.

Darla hurried out of the guest room and stopped dead at the top of the stairs, her eyes round at the sight of him.

"Are you all right?" he demanded. "Come down here, I want to talk to you." The anxiety that had been with him for the past sixty miles drained away at the sight of her standing there, looking so flushed and surprised. But the sudden relief roughened his voice.

Darla lingered at the head of the stairs. "What happened?" she said. "Did you miss your plane?"

He set the luggage down on the thick carpet and stood waiting for her. "First, I want to know if you're okay."

"I'm fine. Of course I'm fine. Why wouldn't I be?"

He didn't let her get away with this small bluff. "I know about the accident," he said.

"Claude told you? That's not fair! He promised he wouldn't say a word!"

Travis felt his sternness slipping away at the sight of her distress. "Come on down," he said, more gently this time. "I couldn't very well fly off to Kansas City not knowing for sure whether you were hurt."

Reluctantly, she began a slow descent. "Claude could have told you that. Or did he think he'd blabbed too much already?"

"Don't blame him." He smiled at her indulgently. "I knew that you intended to drive up to the lodge this afternoon, and I happened to ask him if you got there all right. In spite of any promise he made you, he knew better than to tell me any lies." A hint of grimness returned to his voice.

"I hope he told you that it wasn't my fault." She looked up at him, half cross, half coaxing, her curls slightly damp and her skin as rosy as a baby's.

"All he said was that there had been a little fender bender in the parking lot. He was downright shifty and evasive about the whole thing. So I decided to drive back and see for myself what he was covering up. He wouldn't even give me an estimate of the damages. Just said he couldn't tell."

"Well, he could at least have said that it wasn't my fault!" Darla turned and headed toward the kitchen.

Travis followed, unbuttoning his short shearling coat. "I checked the Porsche as I came in. The left rear fender may have to be replaced. And the taillight's gone, of course."

"Just ask anybody, they'll tell you that it wasn't my fault," she repeated, with a single-mindedness that he recognized from her younger days. "Or, now that you're here, you could ask Jennifer."

"Jennifer?"

"Yes, she'll tell you." Darla put two tall glasses on a tray and found half a carton of soft drinks under the sink. She stopped to look at him speculatively. "You'll like her. She's a friend of Claude's."

"Is that right? And just how friendly do they happen to be?"

"Very friendly. For years and years. Practically since childhood."

He recognized another of her customary tactics, dragging a red herring into the conversation whenever there was something she didn't want to talk about. But he was so relieved to find her perky and well that he resigned himself to postponing discussion of the small accident until she was ready to talk about it. He pretended an interest in this Jennifer person. "If she's a childhood friend of Claude's she must be French. And she's no spring chicken, I bet."

Darla glanced at him in exasperation. "Of course she's not old. You'll love her. She's got the bluest eyes you ever saw."

His mind flashed back to another pair of blue eyes he had encountered that day, and his good mood vanished abruptly.

"I don't want any of that stuff," he said, motioning toward the glasses on the tray.

Darla was noisily scooping ice cubes around. "Oh, this isn't for you. These are for Jennifer and me."

"She's here?" He looked around him. "Where? What's she doing here?"

"We're hot tubbing. I just came in to get us some cold drinks."

"Well, it looks like Claude was pretty tight-lipped after all. He didn't say a word about this old blue-eyed buddy of his moving in here the minute my back was turned."

"Oh, Trav, don't be like that. You're always so suspicious. You know you don't like me to stay alone. And who knew how long you were going to be gone? And Jennifer had no place to stay. Claude was going to take her to a motel."

"He was, was he?" Travis said grimly.

"Yes, he was. But then he had to go and meet you, and it just seemed better all around if she came here."

"And whose idea was that?"

"Why—mine, of course!"

"Are you sure?"

Darla frowned, puzzled. "Claude was going to drive her down to a motel and I said for her to stay with me. That's how it happened."

He looked at her sardonically. "And neither one of them put up much of an argument, I'll bet."

"Couldn't we talk about this later?" she said nervously. She forced a yawn. "Maybe in the morning. It's getting late, and I'm tired. Jennifer's tired, too. She's come a long way, and I'm sure she's anxious to get into bed."

He laughed harshly. "I wouldn't be the least surprised. Has she brought up the subject of the new lodge yet?"

"Of course she hasn't." Darla dismissed the whole subject. "You will be here in the morning, won't you? You're not leaving again tonight?"

"Don't worry, I'll be here," he said decisively.

"Good. Then you and Jennifer can have a nice long talk after breakfast," Darla said. "Now, why don't you go unpack—or fix yourself a nice relaxing drink or something."

He looked at her with sudden inspiration. "Why don't you make one for me, Big Eyes. Get out the bartender's guide and mix me up something special."

Whistling very softly through clenched teeth, Travis left the kitchen. He ran lightly up the stairs, yanking at the knot in his tie. He didn't understand Darla's reasons for keeping the two of them apart until the morning, but he had no intention of waiting that long before confronting Claude's blue-eyed bait.

Chapter Six

Jennifer leaned back against the headrest and stared out into the blackness of the night. The wind had strengthened and was keeping up a steady rush of sound in the trees, like a great breathing animal out there in the dark. Underneath it all, in steady counterpoint, beat the rhythmic chug of the pump that kept the water churning. The indirect lighting was just strong enough to reflect the occasional snowflakes that had begun to eddy beyond her sheltered corner.

A feeling of unreality crept over her. What was she doing in this place? She closed her eyes and tried to order her thoughts, but they kept getting caught up in the noises of the night, each logical progression soon dissolving in mist.

"Well, if it isn't the menace of the mountain!" a deep mocking voice said above her.

Jennifer's head snapped upright, her eyes wide. The tall male figure looming between the steam and the snow had the quality of a hallucination. But the voice—and his wide-shouldered height—were unmistakable. He was wearing a short white terry cloth robe, tightly belted, that left his strong, hard-muscled legs bare to midthigh. He stood looking down at her, apparently oblivious of the cold.

His face was handsome in a rough-hewn way—very broad across the cheekbones. The thick dark hair and slanted heavy eyebrows added to the impression of power and strength that he gave off, but instead of the black stare that the mirrored goggles had led her to expect, his eyes were surprisingly light, a gleaming silver gray in the tan of his face.

Jennifer sank an inch or two deeper into the bubbling water so that it covered her shoulders, then held herself rigidly still. The taunting, almost hostile tone of his voice made her feel even more defenseless in her nakedness. Her first instinct was to cover herself with her hands, but she willed herself to sit quietly, sensing that it would amuse him to see her flutter and squirm. The dimness of the light combined with the frothiness of the water would be a sufficient garment—as long as he stayed where he was.

"I thought you would be happier to see me," he said provocatively.

"Happier to—" She stared up at him in bewilderment. "I don't understand."

"Well, now you won't have to wait so long. You can get right down to business."

"Tonight?" she said doubtfully. He didn't sound as though it was business he had in mind.

"Why not?" Still that provocative tone. "What's wrong with right now?"

Jennifer held his gaze without answering. She certainly had been lulled into a feeling of false security by Darla's airy assurance that her brother would simply come along and take care of everything. Now, here he was—making a major production out of a few car repairs. Well, no doubt you didn't get to be a big tycoon by being free and easy with your money. Finally she said, "I don't happen to have the figures with me."

"But I bet they're not far away, are they? And of course there is the most important one—you've always got that with you...."

His voice was perfectly steady, but what he said made no sense at all.

"Did Darla tell you what happened?" How she would love to see Darla come through the door right now, bearing a robe or a towel—or anything.

"Darla told me all I need to know. I think we can leave her out of this," he said confidently.

"We can?" An ominous thought struck Jennifer. "You are Travis MacKay, aren't you?"

"Don't tell me you have any doubts." He took a step closer, and she shrank deeper into the water. "Perhaps it's time we talked about Claude."

"Claude?" The man was either drunk or crazy. "I don't know what you're talking about."

"Are you trying to tell me that Claude has nothing to do with your being here? That you'd be right where you are even if Claude didn't exist?"

"I'm not trying to tell you anything. I think you'd better go sleep it off."

He smiled, an unexpected flash of white in the darkness of his face.

There was no use talking to him, Jennifer thought. Better to preserve a dignified silence. As dignified as she could manage with no clothes on. No one— ever—was going to hear the story of the schoolgirl fantasy that had brought her here. Especially not this wild man who never saw her except to accuse her, bully her. If she ever got out of this situation, she'd make sure she never had anything more to do with him. In fact, she would hurry in the opposite direction if she so much as glimpsed him on the horizon. But right at the moment she found it impossible to tear her eyes away from the silver-gray ones that bored into her own.

Travis gazed tensely down into her wide sapphire eyes. *Blue enough to drown in,* he thought. Long, dragging seconds passed as he waited for her denial of any connection with Claude, not realizing how keenly he'd hoped for one until it was not forthcoming.

He smothered his disappointment with anger. Very well, then. If she was here to influence his decision to expand Highlands, let her earn her money. Or whatever coin Claude was paying her in. He had been expecting something like this from the Frenchman, but he had never dreamed that Claude would be able to find the one person who could overcome his own defenses. How could she look at him like that—as though she had stars in her eyes instead of dollar signs?

Well, he thought grimly, perhaps it was time to see how good she was at her chosen profession. He yanked at his belt to loosen it.

In spite of her resolve to stand on her dignity, Jennifer inhaled sharply as his robe fell open.

He gave her a savage smile. "No doubt you expected me to be the decadent type who parades around naked in front of his kid sister. Sorry to disappoint you.''

He tossed the robe on the bench, and she saw he was wearing brief black swimming trunks. He was all lean muscle, with a narrow waist and flat, ridged stomach, and he moved with the grace and power of an athlete.

An echo of her conversation with Darla came into her head as he turned toward her. He was like a magnificent animal, strong and lithe as a lion. A black-maned lion with a tawny golden body. A fully awake prowling lion, with a definite glint in his eye.

As he stepped into the swirling water, she held herself poised ready for action, not knowing what he would do next. She saw his eyes widen as he took in her nudity. The humorless smile twisted his lips again as he settled back onto a seat opposite her.

The instant his weight was off his feet, she surged upright. The swirling waters dragged at her, trailing in long rivulets down her flawlessly smooth skin. She made no fluttery futile efforts to cover herself with her hands, but kept her body sideways to him as she quickly and steadily climbed the steps out of the hot tub—out of his reach.

Travis took in the perfect circle of her proud rosy-tipped breast, the long tapered back, the sweet curve of the hips and the slender, elegant legs. Then she snatched up his robe and flung it around her shoulders.

Jennifer never looked back. She clutched the robe around her, barely aware of the icy air against the exposed parts of her body and of the cold of the redwood planking on her bare feet. She took long strides, head up, carefully not running. At last she reached the door that opened into the house—and sanctuary.

Once inside, she resisted the temptation to slam the door behind her. Instead, she closed it very carefully. Then she leaned back against it, quite breathless but feeling that she had escaped with at least a few shreds of her dignity intact.

Darla came into the hallway carrying two tall glasses filled with dark liquid on a tray and an oversize yellow bath towel over her arm. She looked at Jennifer with round eyes.

"Oh, did Trav bring you out a robe?" she asked.

Jennifer hastily thrust her arms through the terry cloth sleeves, enveloped herself in its white folds and tied the belt as tightly as it would go. She cast an appraising eye back at the door. It would be very satisfying to lock him out—to let him parboil for a while and hope it might soak out some of whatever devil was inside him. But with Darla here, that wouldn't work. And probably there was no use wishing for a whip and a chair, either.

"I thought Trav would be up in his room telephoning. That's usually where he is ten minutes after he gets home," Darla went on. "I'd have been out sooner, but I had to go get my bikini on."

"That *is* your brother?" said Jennifer.

"Yes, that's Travis." Darla looked puzzled. "Didn't he introduce himself?"

"No. Somehow we didn't get around to that. I thought he was supposed to be in Kansas City."

"On a plane to Kansas City," Darla corrected her. "But old Claude went and let it out of the bag about the accident, and Trav came steaming back to see for himself if I was all right."

"Very brotherly of him, I'm sure," Jennifer said dryly. "So he knows all about me—about my car?"

"No, not yet. He just wasn't in the right mood to hear about that. I wish everybody wouldn't keep *rushing* me. He wasn't supposed to be back for days—and I haven't had time to figure out the right way to tell him."

Jennifer thought of saying, "Just march right out there, young lady, and tell your brother in plain English that you were driving too fast and skidded on the ice and smashed up my nice new car." She bit back the words. She didn't know what was bothering Travis MacKay, but he obviously wasn't fit to be spoken to right now. Perhaps a night's sleep would sober him up—or calm him down.

Darla apparently saw the softening in her eyes. "I'll tell him in the morning," she promised fervently.

"The very first thing in the morning," Jennifer said sternly.

"Well, right after breakfast," Darla compromised. "Trav's a bear until he's had his bacon and eggs."

Chapter Seven

Jennifer woke to see gray light seeping into the big bedroom around the heavy draperies at the window. She stretched luxuriously in the king-size bed. She had expected to soak her pillow with tears last night. Instead she had gone to sleep at once and slept dreamlessly. No, not quite dreamlessly. There had been something about lions, but she felt too lazy to try to recapture it now.

Perhaps she had been too emotionally exhausted to cry over Claude last night—but she didn't feel like doing it this morning either. A brief uneasiness stirred deep inside her at the fickleness of her own emotions, but she yawned and suppressed it.

The straight chair was still in place where she had put it last night, the back braced underneath the doorknob. Ready for a siege, just in case the strange Mr. MacKay got any more ideas in the night.

The house was profoundly still. It must be very early in the morning; that gray light would be the first sign of dawn. She groped for her watch on the bedside table. It said nine thirty-four. She shook it unbelievingly.

She rose and opened the curtains to a world of snow. The dense whiteness filled the air and blanketed the hillside that sloped away in front of her, adding more inches to the many that had already accumulated, deadening every sound.

Jennifer padded into the bathroom in her bare feet to look for her robe. It hung over the tub where Darla had left it the night before, both sleeves hopelessly shriveled from their encounter with the hot water. Jennifer wondered impudently whether she should just swagger out with Mr. MacKay's terry cloth robe over her old-fashioned nightgown—a flannel gown that was a perfect copy of her great-grandmother's, except that it barely reached mid-thigh. For a moment she was tempted—then surprised at herself that the thought would even cross her mind—but decided that it would be too much like waving a red flag at a bull. And anyway, her slippers were still out on the deck. A terry cloth robe with Texas boots would spoil the effect.

There was still another robe in her overnight case: a filmy peignoir of blue and silver silk that floated around her as she walked. She had bought it in a Dallas shop so exclusive that the garments had individual names. This particular one was called Moonlight. Whatever had she been thinking of? Jennifer shook her head to clear it; she didn't want to think about that right now.

She pulled on her jeans and the white silk shirt from yesterday, promising herself that the first thing she was going to do was to get her suitcase out of the Porsche and change her clothes. Well, maybe the second thing. She was gloriously hungry. Last night's lack of appetite had disappeared with a vengeance. So much for mourning over Claude, she thought ruefully; what a fickle character I am. Instead of tragic, she felt eager—almost giddy—and as free and alive as if she were seventeen again. Perhaps it was a reaction of some kind. Right now she wasn't going to be bothered with worrying about it. She pulled on her boots and braced herself to go out and beard the lion.

The door to the master bedroom was closed. Darla's door was open, but the room was empty and the bed unmade with clothes strewn around in disarray.

Jennifer walked down the carpeted stairs, moving quietly in harmony with the mood of the house, the empty rooms, the thickly falling snow outside the windows.

In the living room she stopped, her attention caught by the telephone on the table. She could call Claude, have him come and get her out of here. She giggled. She could tell him that his banker was bonkers. The phone number of the lodge slid into her mind as smoothly as though she called it every day of her life. She lifted the receiver. Before it was halfway to her ear, she heard a remembered voice, terse and staccato, rapping out orders to some unfortunate on the other end. Travis MacKay was laying down the law to one of his subordinates. Jennifer hung up carefully.

The apricot-colored refrigerator purred quietly to itself in the kitchen. Empty soft drink cans stood on the countertop, the only signs of human occupation except for the note in the center of the table. That sprawling, exuberant handwriting had to be Darla's.

Sleepyheads,
We're going to have the most wonderful breakfast when I get back from the store. Where's the nearest place to find caviar? Just kidding—

Jennifer glanced from the unsigned note in her

hand to the snow piling up outside the window. How long ago had Darla written this? How long had she been gone?

Jennifer opened the side door and stepped into the chill of the garage. A gray Mercedes was sitting there by itself. The Porsche was gone. She had to struggle with the heavy garage door to pull it up. Snow was banking against it with alarming speed. A light but persistent wind swirled fat snowflakes to melt in her hair and on her clothes as she stepped outside. Tire tracks leading from the Porsche's side of the garage were barely visible, and filling in rapidly as she watched.

Feeling helpless, she went back to the kitchen. She read the note again, trying to force some recollection of a door shutting, a car leaving sometime earlier in the morning. But there was nothing in her memory to give a clue to the time Darla had left.

She heard no sound, but something in the atmosphere changed, the air became charged, and she knew he was in the doorway behind her. She turned sharply to face him, thrusting the note at him in lieu of a greeting.

He put out his hand to take it. Their eyes locked. Their fingers touched. Jennifer felt the jolt of his touch strike into the center of her being. Her heart beat faster, her breathing was suddenly obstructed. His sudden rigidity told her that he felt it, too. Then his eyes left hers and everything in the room seemed to shift slightly out of focus, leaving her standing in unfamiliar territory.

He read the note at a glance, and the light-gray eyes came back to her face. "Do you know when she left?"

Jennifer shook her head. "I just woke up a few minutes ago. From the look of the tire tracks, she must have been gone for quite a while. Didn't you hear her, either?"

He pushed up the sleeve of his gray sweatshirt to look at his watch. "I've been on the phone to Kansas City for almost an hour and a half. She must have gone well before then. I didn't hear a thing until the garage door went up just now. That was you, I suppose."

"Yes. I came down and found the note, so I checked on the Porsche and found it gone."

He looked out the window at the densely falling snow. "Where's the nearest store? What direction would she go?"

"I'm not sure. Government Camp, maybe?"

"Government Camp is twelve or fifteen miles from here. She never got that far in this weather."

"Not in that shiny red toy of a car!" Jennifer flared up suddenly. "I suppose you bought her that."

"She wanted a Porsche, I bought her a Porsche," he said harshly. "I didn't ask for your opinion on a suitable car for my sister."

"You're going to get it, anyway." The hot blood was coursing through her veins; anger would have to do as an outlet. "She wanted a new toy and you got it for her. But there are shiny toys and shiny toys, and a red sports car is the last thing someone like Darla needs."

"What do you mean, 'someone like Darla'?" he said ominously.

"Someone with so much reckless abandon and disregard of consequences. With the utter confidence that she can't get into anything that Travis can't get her out of."

"I don't consider Darla either reckless or abandoned."

"That's not what I meant. She's heedless, more than anything else. Lovable, but not responsible." Jennifer threw up her hands in exasperation.

The telephone on the wall rang.

Travis reached it in two long strides. "Darla? Where are you? Are you all right?"

"You finally got off the phone!" Darla's cheerful voice sang over the wires. Jennifer could hear her clearly from where she stood.

"Are you all right?" he repeated insistently.

"I'm fine. The Porsche is in the ditch, but I'm perfectly okay. *Everybody's* in the ditch, Trav. The highway is littered with abandoned cars. I'm safe and sound here at the Highway 26 Market, and I only had to walk about a quarter of a mile. Wasn't that lucky?"

"You wait there and I'll be down to get you."

"I don't think even you could make it down here, Trav," Darla replied. "It was just a fluke that I got this far, and that was hours ago. All the roads are blocked. And a truck just slid into a snowplow down below us. Isn't it exciting!"

"You stay right where you are, then," he said reluctantly.

"Oh no, Trav, it's no fun to be snowed in all day at a *grocery store*. Some of the ski instructors are here and we're all going to go on up to the lodge now."

"Stay where you are, Darla."

"The snowplow, the one in the wreck, just came down from there, so the road's cleared for a few minutes, and the boys have a four-wheel drive—and shovels. They can't wait any longer, so I have to go now. The groceries are here on the counter. Sorry I couldn't get back with them. Bye, Trav."

The click of the broken connection was very final. Travis put the receiver back on the hook, but kept his hand on it.

"What's the number of the lodge?" he rapped out.

Jennifer recited it automatically. He gave her an unfathomable look as he punched in the numbers.

"This is Travis MacKay. Get me Claude," he said curtly when the switchboard answered.

It took some time for Claude to be located. While they waited they both stood as motionless as painted figures, the air between them crackling with electric tension.

Claude's voice cut across the emotional current as cheerfully as Darla's had. "Travis! What a grand blizzard! We may not be able to open as we planned—but when we do, what a snowpack we will have!"

"Claude, Darla's on her way up to the lodge with some of your harebrained ski instructors. They're coming up from Highway 26, and I want you to watch out for her. Send a snowmobile down to pick them up."

"A snowmobile? Yes, perhaps that would be best. I will let you know when they are here safely."

"Good. And Claude, what are the chances of getting my road plowed so I can get out of here?"

"Very poor, I'm afraid. The main roads are nearly impassible already. The secondary and private roads are far down on the highway department's list of priorities."

"It's vitally important that I get the next plane out of here to Kansas City."

There was a discreet silence on the other end of the line.

"All right," said Travis, finally. "Let me know when Darla gets there."

As he hung up, he consulted his watch again. "I'll go up and call Kansas City again—tell them I might not make it. You can let me know when breakfast is ready."

"Let's get one thing straight," said Jennifer. "You don't seem to realize it, but I didn't come here to be responsible for your breakfast."

His momentary preoccupation with business vanished, and he brought his entire attention to bear on her. "Is that a fact?" he said. "Tell me, Jennifer, what exactly *did* you come here to be responsible for?"

Chapter Eight

I'm here to see that I get my car back—in the same condition it was in when I drove it to Highlands," Jennifer said.

"Your car? What car?"

"The car Darla smashed into in the parking lot at the lodge." Travis was looking at her as uncomprehendingly as if she had suddenly begun speaking Chinese. He was so completely nonplussed that Jennifer began to enjoy herself. She leaned back against the kitchen table and went on. "The car you would have heard about last night, if Darla hadn't been determined to wait for just the right moment to tell you about it. Or that you would have heard about early this morning—if you weren't such a bear in the morning before you have your bacon and eggs. That's why she plunged out into the storm to bring in the groceries. I didn't think she would take the Porsche, though. Not after promising Claude that she wouldn't.''

Travis shook his head like a punch-drunk fighter. ''Start at the beginning,'' he said. ''Tell me the whole story.''

By the time she finished, his expression had gone from endearingly bewildered back to woodenly unreadable.

Jennifer wished she could see just what was happening to her own expression. She had the strange feeling that her mind was operating—or not operating—on two distinct levels. She was aware of her usual voice going on talking about black ice and car doors, while all the time a smaller voice inside her head was saying gay giddy things like: ''Those *are* little laugh lines at the corner of his eyes, they definitely are,'' and ''That is the greatest, the sexiest lower lip—'' Jennifer was having more and more trouble concentrating on what she was saying. His mouth was wide and firm, but not thin-lipped. In fact, it was just right. Perfect....

Presently her voice, the one they both could hear, faltered to a stop. The house was soundless. Even the refrigerator was still. The world seemed blanketed in stillness, a quiet that cocooned them, isolating them from everything around them. Jennifer was aware only of him.

He was standing in front of her, only a few feet away. But that was too far; the irresistible force that was drawing them together would not tolerate it. After what seemed an eternity he stepped forward. He put his hand on her arm.

She felt the warmth of his touch through the thin silk, and all of her nerve endings leaped to life, begging for more. Her body longed—no, it *lusted* for the feel of his hand on her bare skin. She stood as motionless as a statue while wild fantasies flashed through her mind. The wretched shirt, how she hated it, a barrier between herself and her mounting desire. She pictured it being slowly unbuttoned, being eased away from her shoulders, leaving her gloriously exposed to this new world of passion she had never before explored. No, let it be *torn* away, let it be ripped from the body that only wanted to be free of it....

Nothing had prepared Jennifer for the unexpected force of her feelings. She was simultaneously terrified and exultant. It was like drowning. Like being struck by lightning. It was as if her whole body were captive, driven, shuddering under some power beyond her control.

Travis felt her tremble under his hand, and knew he was defeated. Whoever she was, she was all he had ever wanted. He had to have her. Whatever it cost him, in either money or self-respect.

He reached out and Jennifer came to him blindly, eyes closed, lips slightly parted. The roughness of his embrace was partly the urgency of the desire that rose within him, partly hot resentment directed at her and at Claude and all their manipulations. He crushed his lips down upon hers. But the softness, the sweetness, the feel of her body pressed against his—all conspired to steal away his anger. He had almost surrendered it completely when the telephone rang.

They both stood rigid as the shrill sound ripped through the room, shattering the mood irretrievably. Travis raised his head, but his arms around her did not loosen their hold until the insistent summons rang out a second time.

Shocked back into harsh reality, he put her away from him roughly, turning his back on her as he took down the receiver and muttered a savage acknowledgment into the mouthpiece.

"Travis? This is Claude. When we spoke before, I neglected to ask you about Miss Ericson. Is she on her way to the lodge with Darla?"

"No," Travis said shortly. "She's still here."

"May I speak with her, then?"

He thrust the receiver at her wordlessly and stalked to the far end of the room, into the dining area. There he stood, staring moodily out the big windows at the vista that was nearly obscured by the thickly falling snow.

Jennifer's mind was whirling from having taken the sudden plunge into fantasy and then having been so abruptly dropped back to earth. She murmured a weak word of greeting into the telephone.

"Chérie," Claude said, "I was hoping you would come here. But perhaps it is best that you are not out in the storm."

"Yes," she answered, distracted, hardly listening.

"When the weather clears, the skiing will be glorious."

"I suppose so."

"It looks as though, for the next day or two, a handful of us will be camped out here at the lodge. It will be an adventure. It would be perfect if you were here to share it."

"Yes," Jennifer said again, lying politely. How excruciating it would have been to be snowed in with Claude now that she knew her feelings for him had died. She cast a hasty glance at Travis's back. But what in the world was it going to be like to be snowed in with *him*?

"We have our own generator here, of course," Claude was saying. "For the lights and heat. I understand the MacKay house also has an emergency generator, so you need not worry if the wires are down temporarily."

"That's good," she said absently, still only half listening. Her attention was focused on Travis. She wondered what made him stand there so rigidly. Perhaps he was getting a better hold on his senses and was embarrassed at where a momentary lapse had led him.

"Some think that the loss of electricity can be most romantic," Claude continued. "Being cut off from the world with the firelight and a single candle. But it is my experience that one can always turn down the lamps. And romance in front of the fireplace is only improved when the furnace is also running." There were muffled voices in the background. When he spoke again, it was with regret. "I must go now, *chérie*."

"Yes," she said. "Goodbye, Claude." She hung up.

Travis turned to face her. It had been a singularly unrevealing conversation from this end—nothing but a few words of agreement from her. Claude would probably shoot himself if he knew how untimely his interruption had been. Not that it would matter in the long run, he told himself with bleak honesty.

They were locked in here together for Lord only knew how long. There would be plenty of time for him to lose his grip on himself again. And it probably wouldn't take him long with her looking at him like that, so vulnerably and tenderly.

Jennifer's thoughts were in confusion. Claude's call had been a very timely interruption. Nothing like this had ever happened to her before, and she still felt as if she hadn't recovered her breath—or her wits. There was something to be said for the days when women carried smelling salts around with them. She certainly could use something to jolt her brain back into working order. Not liquor, though. She was far too intoxicated as it was. She blushed as she recalled the wild abandon of her thoughts only a scant few minutes ago.

Travis consulted his wristwatch again. "I have to let Kansas City know that I won't be coming," he said, with careful, almost formal politeness. "After that—" He paused to rephrase his words. "When I come down again, perhaps we should check the food supplies and see just what we have to live on for the next day or so."

Once he had left the room, Jennifer sat down abruptly in a kitchen chair. Food was the farthest thing from her mind. What was happening to her? She had never experienced such an explosion of sensuality in her own body. No other man's touch had ever affected her so. No other kisses. In other days she could remember thinking during a kiss, "Yes, this one is very nice—but he isn't Claude." But now that seemed like something out of a previous life.

Now that she had accepted her vision of Claude for what it was—nothing more than an adolescent's dream—all her defenses were down. It was possible that all this was just a reaction, she reasoned. Yes, that must be it. The attentions of any attractive man would probably have sparked the same irrational response in her. She was going to have to accept that she was basically an emotionally fickle person. Be clearheaded about this, Jennifer told herself fiercely. Don't make the mistake of getting fixated on the very first man you encounter after shedding your obsession with Claude.

Emotionally this was the worst possible time to be shut up alone with any man, much less this one. Therefore, she was just going to have to keep in mind that any feeling on her part would be purely physical, temporary and essentially meaningless. Yes, she must look on it as a game, and try to play it as one—as lighthearted a game as she could manage to make it.

With that resolution firmly in mind, Jennifer stood. Looking around her, she decided to search the cupboards. She found four different sets of dishes, from informal earthenware decorated with painted daisies to fine translucent white china. Apparently no one in this house needed to eat off the same kind of dish more than two days a week unless he or she wanted to. The spice cabinet was completely stocked, the bread box empty. The two sets of flatware were of stainless steel; evidently even rich people drew the line at leaving valuable silver lying around unattended in an empty house.

There were five cans of diet soda under the sink, along with two cans of dog food. Perhaps the oilman who had borrowed the house last August had brought a dog. There didn't seem to be any sign of one in the MacKay family. Jennifer stood up with a can in each hand and placed them prominently in view on the counter. Let him think he was going to get dog food for breakfast. After all, it was supposed to be wholesome enough. Not tasty, maybe, but snowbound travelers couldn't expect pheasant under glass. For no good reason she could think of she felt her spirits rising. She was beginning to feel as if she were on some kind of emotional express elevator with no one at the controls.

It would have been nice to find some coffee, but there was none, only a handful of tea bags forgotten in a canister. She encountered two more small containers; the oilman's cook apparently had not found it worthwhile to pack up half a can of baking powder and a small jar of olives.

Jennifer found herself listening for any sound from upstairs as she read the labels on three jars of imported marmalade. She strained to hear an opening door, a footfall on the stairway. He moved lightly for a big man. It would be easy for him to take her by surprise again. She wanted to have plenty of warning the next time, so that she could have herself under control and be calm and composed when he came into the room. She felt a tremor at the thought, and knew that sane and sensible behavior was probably out of the question.

Could she somehow explain to him that a crazy infatuation had just gone out of her life, had exploded and vanished in an instant, leaving her so shocked and vulnerable that she simply wasn't rational right now? Could she ask him if he would kindly take whatever was happening between them for what it was—some kind of aberration that would most likely vanish any minute? Love had turned out to be such an undependable will-o'-the-wisp that she would always be expecting it to go up in a puff of smoke—if she ever left herself open to it again. Which she had not the slightest intention of doing.

She wouldn't allow herself to fall in love—or even into infatuation—for a long, long time. Not until she could trust her emotions to be on some kind of an even keel. And then there would probably have to be a long engagement—years, maybe—before she could be sure that this time it was the real, lasting thing. All these years she had been certain she knew whom she loved, and look where that had got her. Jennifer felt the tears prick her eyelids as she mourned her lost certainty.

She pulled open the door of the big freezer and stared blindly at the sparsely laden shelves.

"I remembered I had instant coffee in my suitcase. Sometimes I don't want to be bothered with room service."

Jennifer spun around. After one revealing moment of surprise—their eyes locking for just the space of a heartbeat—she quickly averted her gaze. She reached out and took the half-full jar of instant coffee from his hand, being careful not to let her fingers touch his strong brown ones.

Travis had been feeling quite buoyed up at being able to provide coffee, but one glimpse of her unhappy face brought him down again.

"Look, it isn't so bad," he said quickly. "Even if we happened to be snowed in here for several days, we wouldn't starve. It may not be exactly a balanced diet, but there seems to be enough food to keep us going. And in a pinch, we can fall back on the dog food," he added, hoping for a smile.

Jennifer turned away from him, aimlessly brushed her long dark hair back from her shoulders and tried to get a grip on herself. "Yes," she agreed, a little shakily, "and there's more than enough marma-lade." This was going to be worse than she'd thought. His mere presence was making her light-headed. Or could that be hunger? She opened the coffee jar and made a production of finding two spoons and two cups, clattering them down ner-vously on the terra-cotta countertop. He was al-ready running hot water out of the tap. After the instant coffee had been measured and stirred into both cups, he slid them into the microwave oven for the few seconds it took to make them steam invit-ingly.

How natural and domestic he can be, Jennifer mused. How companionable! She buried her face in the steam from the cup he'd handed her and reined in her runaway thoughts. Only trouble lay in that direction. Nonetheless, as he gazed out the window at the white-on-white vista outside, she stole an-other look in his direction.

He was wearing running shoes and jeans and a blue plaid shirt of fine lightweight wool, and he didn't look at all like a financier or banker or what-ever it was he was supposed to be. The shirt was un-buttoned at the throat, exposing smooth bronzed skin and the strong column of his neck. Her eyes lifted and lingered on his thick, unruly brown hair. It curled invitingly at the nape of his neck, and she had a sudden urge to lay her hand there, to feel the crispness of the hair, the warmth of his skin. She was suddenly sharply aware of her own body, the whisper of her clothes against her own skin.

I'm going to have to start pinching myself, Jennifer thought. *Or taking cold showers.* The man was positively uncanny. She wondered if he had the same effect on all women. Maybe he did, and that was why he'd never felt the need to cultivate good manners. Though he was being polite enough at the moment. And that was exactly what the moment called for—careful politeness. She would try some of it herself.

"I saw a package of frozen waffles in the freezer somewhere," she said. "That's the only thing that even looks like breakfast. But there's no butter or syrup to put on them."

He opened the freezer door and shook his head. "I'm afraid that breakfast is a lost cause. It's after eleven already. Shall we just skip it and proceed directly to lunch?" He stepped back as though leaving the decision to her.

"Someone seems to have been very fond of frozen cheesecake," she said, as she took a couple of packages. He was standing between her and the counter, so it was only natural to place the boxes in his waiting hands—being very careful not to let their fingers touch, of course, and turning away quickly. "That doesn't seem to be in keeping with the low-calorie dinners on the bottom shelf."

"No, it doesn't," Travis agreed. "Maybe one of the party was compulsive about counting calories and didn't trust the houseboy not to slip in a dollop of butterfat when she wasn't looking."

Jennifer handed him two trays of veal parmigiana. Belatedly she realized that he would need much more nourishment than that, and reached for the first things that came to hand, the last package of lasagna and a box of frozen huckleberries.

He accepted them without question and turned away to start opening the cardboard containers. Free of his gaze, she was able to consider the food situation with a little more composure.

"Your oilman friend must have enjoyed fishing for trout more than he enjoyed eating them," she said lightly. "There must be four or five dozen of them in here."

"Perhaps he thought he was leaving me a delicacy." Travis manipulated the microwave as neatly as if he did it every day instead of being practically a stranger in his own kitchen. "Personally I'd rather have salmon, but trout can be pretty good, too. Shall we have trout for dinner?"

"There's nothing to fry them in," she said, practically, "but I suppose they can be broiled. After they're defrosted." Taking a double handful of the small frozen fish out of the freezer, she spread them in the sink and stood looking down at them reflectively. "We used to fish for trout here—my father and I. He liked Rimrock Lake and Lost Lake. If we were lucky and caught them quickly in the cool of the morning, we'd fry them up, and they were the best tasting fish in the whole world."

Fishing seemed like a nice, safe topic of conversation so she went on doggedly. "But if it took us all day to catch enough, then the first ones weren't so good. Out of the water and into the pan, that's the best. Freezing isn't so good for fish, either. You lose a lot of the flavor...." Her voice trailed off.

"You're a local girl?" The gray eyes were unreadable again.

"I was. I've been away for a long time. In Texas, mostly."

"So you came all the way from Texas," Travis said musingly. He was trying to figure out the mechanics of her being here. Claude hadn't known just when he and Darla would be coming to Highlands. But he'd known they'd be here as soon as possible, once the lodge was open for the season. Therefore it would be only practical to have Jennifer on the premises, ready for action at the first opportunity.

Claude always seemed to have on hand an inexhaustible supply of young women for whatever job was currently vacant here—like the cool blonde who'd done the cooking last spring. And the high-fashion blonde who'd decorated the house. Both of whom had let him know in not-too-subtle ways that they were available for other things. He'd been mildly amused at the time; Claude had played his cards, and Travis had ignored them. But now Claude had brought in a long-legged brunette with eyes blue enough to drown in, and suddenly the stakes—the very game itself—had changed beyond recognition.

"What do you think of the plans for expanding Highlands?" he said abruptly.

"What?" She looked confused by the sudden change of subject. "Highlands? I think Claude started to say something about that, but I don't remember what it was."

How convincing she sounded. But he was well aware that no one at Highlands thought or talked of anything but the plans for the new resort. She was probably some out-of-work actress that Claude had rehearsed well in her new part.

Everything about him had changed somehow, Jennifer thought. For a few minutes he had seemed almost nice. *Really* nice. For a few minutes she had been thinking of him as domestic and companionable—and now his prowling-lion glint was back again. The telephone rang beside her. Without thinking, she put out her hand and answered it.

"I called before, but Travis was on the phone," Darla's high, happy voice announced. "We're all here safe and sound and the weather report says it's going to snow for days!''

"Days?'' Jennifer repeated, a sinking feeling inside her.

"Well, today and tonight, anyway. Maybe more. Listen, are you two okay? Will you have enough to eat?''

"You saw what was in the freezer.'' Jennifer was trying to adjust her thoughts to the possibility of being stuck in this house for days.

Travis put out his hand for the receiver, his lordly, commanding hand, and because there was no warmth in the silver-gray eyes, something flared inside her. Haughtily she stepped back.

"Darla,'' she said, "did you by any chance take my suitcase and camera cases out of the Porsche and put them somewhere before you drove off this morning?''

"Oh, gee, Jennifer—''

Darla's stricken tone of voice did not melt Jennifer's heart this time. "You mean that all my worldly goods are in a ditch along the highway somewhere?''

"I'm sorry, Jennifer. But don't worry, Trav will take care of everything.''

"I'm not so sure about that. Do you realize that the only clothes I have to wear are just what I'm standing up in?''

"Go up to my room and help yourself," Darla said generously.

"I very much doubt that anything there would fit me."

"I brought a ton of sweaters. Great big ones, some of them. Try them, I'm sure you'll find something. Oh, I know," Darla said with relief. "Trav has a nifty new wool shirt. Try that pulled tight with one of my belts. It'll look great on you."

Jennifer was staring at the opposite wall, studiously avoiding looking at Travis, but she remembered vividly enough that he was wearing the shirt under discussion right now. All at once, everything was too much for her. Her indignation and energy seemed to run out together. Wordlessly, she handed the receiver to Travis without looking at him. Now it was her turn to stalk down to the big windows and stare bleakly out at the storm.

After what seemed an eternity, she heard the telephone slam into its cradle.

"Darla sent you a message," he said in a cold, hard voice. "She says that Claude sends his love. And he's sure that you have nothing to worry about."

Chapter Nine

They looked at each other for a long tense moment, the air between them crackling with unspoken questions. Then the oven chimed a message that the first TV dinner was cooked.

"I have a telephone call to make," Travis said and strode from the room.

Jennifer watched him leave, feeling the turmoil of conflicting emotions inside her. The strongest of them was surprise. What in the world had set him off this time? she wondered. Anger and resentment blazed up fiercely, hotly, giving way to relief with a tinge of regret. For a brief moment it had seemed that they had reached some kind of a truce, that they were about to have a peaceful lunch together, a domestic interlude in their stormy relationship. Small chance of that, Jennifer decided crossly. He was about as domestic as a bear with a sore head.

Sitting by herself at the polished maple table, she ate the hot TV dinner. There was no point in cooking the other one until he made up his mind to come down again. He must be developing quite a brisk appetite by now, judging by her own hunger pangs. Her dish was already empty, and though the meal claimed to provide three hundred calories, it hadn't satisfied her in the least. She eyed the cheesecakes hungrily. They were still too solid to cut. Suddenly she was obsessed with the idea of cheesecake; she had to have one and have it now. She slid the package into the microwave oven and heated it in short, ten-second bursts. Finally, while it was still half frozen, she ate it, ate the whole thing, polishing off every last crumb and feeling triumphantly wicked.

Her hunger assuaged, Jennifer wondered what she was going to do for something to wear. If he weren't so completely impossible, she could ask to borrow one of his shirts, a T-shirt, anything. But that was out of the question. And it wasn't likely that she would find anything to fit her own tall and slender body among Darla's belongings. Still, she'd better go up and have a look.

As she climbed the stairs, she was careful not to be careful. She had no intention of being a timid little mouse, tiptoeing around outside his door so as not to rouse the lion. *Let* him explode. Last night she'd had no choice but to run away. But this time was different. This time they would have it out. She was the injured party under this roof, and if he got up on his high horse one more time—well, she didn't know yet exactly what she would say, but whatever it turned out to be, it would involve a whole lot of pointed remarks and plain truths.

Darla had tossed some of her things in the dresser drawers, and Jennifer found a sweater among them that indeed looked like a one-size-fits-all. It was medium blue with a wide slit neckline. Jennifer tried it on, but no matter how she adjusted it, it left one shoulder bare, as it was no doubt designed to do. Planting her booted feet apart, she put her hands on her hips as she studied the effect in the mirror. It was the only garment she could find to wear, so she would wear it, although it was definitely not what she would have chosen under the circumstances—not *these* circumstances. Not with him radiating anger at her as he had in the kitchen and shutting himself up in his room for no apparent reason. Now, if things had only been as they were when he had touched her, kissed her.... She imagined the caress of his hand on the bared shoulder, the touch of his lips....

Enough of that. Turning abruptly away from the mirror, she picked up Darla's scattered clothes and made the bed before going back to her own room. Once there, she gathered up her blouse and some underthings and took them into her bathroom to rinse them out in the basin. As she hung them over the shower rod, she could feel her unpredictable spirits begin to rise again.

Travis sat in his bedroom with a dead telephone in his hand. Somewhere on the mountain a tree limb must have fallen under its burden of snow and taken down the telephone wires. Now the two of them were completely cut off from the outside world.

He was still very angry, but now his anger was directed at himself. He had accepted her for what she was—a beautiful blue-eyed snare. And then he had forgotten about it, totally and completely—until Claude's calculated words of encouragement to her had brought it all back again. And what was worse, if he had to do it again, he knew it was not the treacherous kiss that he would eliminate but his own furious exit. She had shaken him to the core of his being. Whatever web she'd woven, he was well and truly caught.

He could hear her moving around next door and then going back into her own room. He stood up with sudden resolution. He couldn't sit here all day like a sulky teenager. Besides, he was getting damnably hungry.

He passed her open door, heard her humming softly to herself as she worked. It was an unfamiliar tune, but cheerful. He went downstairs, feeling more cheerful himself.

He ate veal and lasagna and cheesecake, finishing everything down to the last crumb just as Jennifer had done. Outside, the wind was blowing harder than before, driving the snow before it so thickly that he could scarcely see a hundred feet from the house. The sky, the whole world was the bleak gray-white of early dawn. The world outside had become threatening, but inside, everything was bright and warm, quiet except for the distant rumble of the furnace and the cheerful purr of the refrigerator.

With no warning, all of the lights in the house winked out. All the efficient little domestic noises died instantly, leaving only an ominous stillness that already seemed to foreshadow the unrelieved darkness soon to come.

Travis got to his feet quickly, not sorry to have a definite job to do. He ran lightly up the stairs. Jennifer stood in the doorway of her room, looking out at a hallway that was already so shadowy that he couldn't read the expression on her face.

"Don't worry," he said. "I'll get my boots on and go outside and start the generator."

She was gone when he came back in boots and parka, and he saw no sign of her downstairs. He found it exhilarating to go outside into the storm, to lean against the wind and pit his muscles against deep snow and balky doors. To deal with well-conditioned machinery that sprang obediently to life under his touch. When he returned, going from the fury of the blizzard to the calm air of the house, it was like escaping from the raging power of a hurricane by stepping into the artificial stillness of its eye. He left his snowy boots and parka in the kitchen and walked in his stocking feet onto the deep pile of the carpet.

She was sitting on the hearth in front of the living room fireplace, feeding sticks of kindling into a crackling fire. She had not heard his cat-footed approach, and he stopped for a long, uninterrupted look at her.

The Texas boots had been replaced by low ivory slippers, affording a tantalizing view of slim ankles. The long slender legs in the close-fitting jeans, the curve of the hip up to the narrow waist were all the more disturbing because he remembered only too well how they had looked last night, unveiled. Her hair, like a waterfall of dark silk, reached almost to her waist. And the bared shoulder—well, that was a silken-skinned invitation that no man could be expected to resist.

Not that he was expected to resist it, he reminded himself coldly. How disappointed she would be if he did. She was so obviously his for the taking that the only suspense was in when she would ask for payment. Would she hold out coyly until she had his pledge of backing for the new lodge, or give herself first and wheedle it out of him afterward? Well, there was only one way to find out.

"You make a good fire," he said briskly, striding forward to hold out his hands to the leaping flames.

Jennifer looked up, startled. The sudden impact of meeting those sapphire eyes made his pulse race.

She looked away quickly and hesitated for a moment before she said, "The fire is a comfort, but it's nothing compared to the sight of the lights coming back on again. For the first time, I can agree with Darla when she calls this place a big old barn. I'd hate to try to heat it with just a few fireplaces."

Abandoning all pretense of interest in the fire, he dropped down beside her.

He gazed openly at her exposed ankles, making it so obvious that she could not fail to notice. After a moment she tucked them beneath her a little more firmly, saying, "While you were starting the generator, I went out on the deck to rescue my slippers. They were protected where they were, under the bench, but I went through a deep drift to get to them. The snow was right up over the tops of my boots...."

Her voice trailed away. Travis sat so close that he was almost touching her, close enough to inhale the faint perfume of her hair. He saw the flush that rose to color the smooth tan of her cheeks and knew she was thinking of the same thing he was, of their clash at the hot tub last night and of her own nude retreat. Jennifer averted her face and fed another stick into the flames.

He could feel the tension rising between them, knew that she felt it, too. He let the silence stretch out, a silence more eloquent than any words. All he had to do was just reach out his hand....

A little imp of perversity inside him made him speak. "Would you like to talk about the plans for the new lodge now?" he asked, almost tenderly.

She looked at him then, complete incomprehension widening the blue eyes this time. What an actress she was. Her hand strayed as though unconsciously to the neckline of the borrowed sweater, pulling it tighter on her slender throat.

"I don't know anything about the lodge," she said, after a pause. "I only arrived at Highlands yesterday."

So she was sticking to her story, was she? All right, they would play out this farce to the bitter end.

"Well, then," he said, "perhaps I'd better explain it to you. You see, I happen to own the lease of the land just west of Highlands." He made a broad gesture with his left hand. "And the new lodge—if we decided to go ahead with it—would go in about three hundred yards above the present one. It will be a hotel, really, and a good-sized one." He gave her a sidelong glance. "Of course, you haven't any idea what it would be like, have you?" Without waiting for an answer, he got to his feet. "I know, I'll lay it all out for you. Be back in a second."

Up in his room, away from her, he acknowledged the facts of the situation to himself angrily. He had thought that he could just go ahead and take what she had come here to offer him, but this unfinished business stood between them like a barrier. He snatched up his sketch pad and pencil. Her time for playing the sweet innocent would soon be over.

Chapter Ten

Jennifer piled logs on the fire with abandon. In a million years she would never understand what made that man tick. He was back almost at once, throwing himself down beside her with that air of barely contained anger that bewildered her so. As she watched, he opened the sketchbook to a clean double page and began to draw with swift, savage strokes.

The violent movements of his drawing pencil gradually slowed and grew steadier as he became caught up in what he was doing. Jennifer sat back and watched him, watched the strong capable hands, his rough-hewn features. The fire blazed up brightly, its flickering light creating a little golden oasis around them in the midst of the deepening grayness of the late afternoon. The increased warmth gradually made her hearthside perch uncomfortable. Never taking her eyes from him, she slid down onto the smooth softness of the fur rug. Half sitting, half re-clining, she reached behind her for one of the large brown floor cushions and tugged it quietly into a position where she could lean back against it.

After a while, Travis, too, seemed to become aware of the added heat at his back, and he followed her onto the rug, though without breaking for an in-stant his concentration on what he was doing.

The wind moaned outside. A sudden fierce gust shuddered the broad windows. He continued to sketch with single-focused intensity. Jennifer real-ized what she was seeing demonstrated one of the prime qualities that made him the successful man he was; this ability to fix his attention on the task at hand. What that meant to his business associates she didn't know or care. What it meant to her just now was that she could feast her eyes on him openly, without finding it necessary to disguise her interest.

There were so many small details about him that she hadn't had the chance to appreciate before: the crisp way his dark hair curled back from his broad forehead, the reckless tilt to his black eyebrows that gave him a buccaneering look.... She could picture him in boots, sword in hand, leading piratical raids on Wall Street. He would look magnificent in boots and with a sword. Mentally, she dressed him in tight-fitting black trousers, a full-sleeved white shirt open almost to the waist and a broad-brimmed plumed hat. High boots and a sword at his side. Beautiful.

Then she started in the other direction, first subtracting the white shirt, exposing the wide shoulders and well-muscled chest. That was even better. Now she could see the arms. She didn't care for bulgy muscles just for the sake of muscle, but she did love a good strong arm. And his were just right.

She didn't have to use her imagination entirely to picture what he looked like underneath his clothes, either the cable-knit sweater and blue jeans he wore now, or the swashbuckling outfit she'd imagined him in before. She had seen him just last night. Not quite as uncovered as *she'd* been, but almost. She half closed her eyes in her effort to remember. He had tossed away the white terry cloth robe and stepped into the hot tub—so close she could have touched him. But the picture was distorted by the turmoil of emotions she had felt at the time. It remained hazy, as if she were peering through thick steam, even thicker than the steam that had risen from the hot water into that cold night. She closed her eyes tightly, trying to bring him into focus.

"Don't go to sleep," Travis ordered curtly. "I want you to look at this."

Startled, she opened her eyes wide, and met the full force of his silver stare. It was like being seized by iron hands and held fast, unable to move or breathe. For a long moment it seemed that he was caught up in the same paralysis. The firelight cast unreadable moving shadows across his stern face. Then he broke the contact, roughly thrusting the sketchbook into her hands.

Obediently she bent her head over it, her senses swimming. He waited silently. She could feel the tension in him as she tried to make sense of the marks on the page. At last the pounding in her heart slowed, and the picture swam into focus.

She was looking at a long three-story building with a bold and striking central entryway. The present lodge was recognizable at one side, with a much bigger, squarer structure behind it. A tiny skier was schussing downhill in a spot where she knew that a dense growth of trees still stood—which must mean they intended to add more ski runs. She paused to admire the strict economy of line that managed to convey some of the speed and joy of skiing with only a handful of pencil strokes.

Behind one wing of the proposed hotel, a miniature figure skater glided across the ice of a large rink. Behind the other wing a diver left the board on his way into what appeared to be a near-Olympic-sized swimming pool.

Jennifer was speechless at the sheer scale of the planned development. Mutely she placed a finger on a peaked-roof jumble at the extreme right of the page and looked at him inquiringly.

He moved closer to see where she was pointing. The wide-necked sweater had slipped down on that side, and she felt his breath on her bared shoulder as he answered.

"Those are the condominiums. Seven hundred units."

"Seven hundred...." she echoed faintly.

"There will be over two hundred rooms in the hotel," he said, "as well as convention facilities for two thousand people."

"Two thousand!" She looked again at the sketch, her eyes unbelieving. "But that's huge!" She pointed to a tiny gondola car in the sketch. "Surely you're not serious about building one of those?"

"Yes, indeed. A gondola to the top of Jackdaw Peak. With a restaurant at the upper terminus. And another new ski run coming down." He was involved in explaining it all to her now, making sure she understood every feature. "The square building is the new day lodge, four times the size of the old facility. That will be the number one priority. Then will come the gondola and the ground-breaking for the hotel. Construction on three new ski lifts will start while the other building is going on."

"How—how long will it all take?"

"Two or three years should see most of it completed." He moved back slightly, his eyes searching her face. "Well, that's it. What do you think?"

"I don't know. I'm simply overwhelmed. I had no idea you had such a huge project in mind."

"Of course you didn't." The sardonic edge had returned to his voice. "But now that you do know, I'm sure that you can see that it's a wonderful idea. Isn't that right?"

"I said I don't know." His unwavering silver stare was making her edgy. She looked down at the sketch again, taking in the sheer extent of it. "Don't you have to get permission from the forest service before you can build on the mountain? Would they agree to all of this construction?"

"They've already reviewed the plans. We expect to receive formal approval in a few days. *If* I decide to go ahead with it, of course." He paused, then went on when she didn't reply. "That's why Claude had to go to that forest service meeting yesterday."

Could it be only yesterday she had come here, starry-eyed after the long years of dreaming? Well, it was no wonder that Claude had permitted their first encounter to be interrupted, had felt it necessary to answer his telephone in the middle of a kiss.

She hadn't realized the immensity of his ambition. Would his dream prove any more substantial than hers had been? Jennifer wondered.

These plans would make Highlands a magnificent ski resort, by far the finest on the mountain, the finest for hundreds of miles around. She could imagine what her father's reaction to an expansion like this would have been. It would have been like getting the greatest Christmas present in the world, beyond his wildest dreams. She felt an upsurge of the old affection she had for this place. She had been happy here as a child. It would be nice to tell people "I grew up at Highlands" and know that they would recognize the name, that it would be well-known and highly regarded all over the country. Even though her own dream of Claude had vanished, she harbored no ill will toward him. She only hoped that this dream of his might somehow come true. She would have to be very careful what she said to this man who held the purse strings and the power.

"Well, what do you say?" Once again, Travis appeared strangely eager to hear her opinion.

"What difference does it make what I say? I'm sure you've already made up your mind."

"There's still time to change it. Nothing is final yet. Suppose I left it up to you. What would it be? Yes or no?"

"That would be silly." Jennifer sought refuge from his searching eyes by feigning interest in the sketch again. "I don't know enough about it. I don't even understand what you mean by convention facilities."

"Banquet hall, exhibition rooms, restaurants," he said tersely.

"I suppose—it must be going to cost a fortune."

"It's okay to come right out and ask the price. It's even been published in the newspapers. Just under seventy-four million dollars."

"Seventy-four million dollars!" It seemed a totally unbelievable amount of money. "That's not just a fortune, that's seventy-four fortunes." She was shaking her head, mentally retreating from even the consideration of such a foolhardy outlay. Another thought struck her. "Do you actually *have* seventy-four million dollars to invest in this—this gamble?"

He uttered an unexpected shout of laughter. "A financier doesn't operate quite like that. My job is to 'find' the money, not to invest my own."

She stared at him, not understanding.

"First we get the state to clear the way to use tax-free revenue bonds to underwrite a substantial portion of the cost. In this case, forty-five million dollars of it. Then I go to work to find a buyer for those bonds. I don't buy them myself. The rest of the money will come from investors wanting to get in on the condominium construction.''

Jennifer looked down at the plans again, seeing them in a new light, in a seventy-four million dollar perspective. No matter what he said, this was no vague project that could be called off on any whim of hers. He must have already made a sizable investment. He would have paid out a large sum for the lease of the land, for having these plans drawn up and for buying this house. If the forest service was agreeing to the land use and the state was going to furnish the bonds to pay for more than half of it, then Travis wasn't honestly going to act on her opinion, no matter what he said. He was just fishing for compliments, trying to impress her with all this million-dollar talk. Or he was making a fool of her; only a fool would believe that *her* verdict would make the difference between going ahead with this or calling it off. This was his way of toying with her. He must be laughing his head off behind that so serious facade. What an actor he was.

"Well?" he prompted again.

"Let me see." She searched the sketch for inspiration. Surprisingly, she found it. "Look," she said, "I don't understand how you're going to handle a convention of two thousand people if you only have two hundred bedrooms in your hotel."

Silently, he reached over and tapped his forefinger on the condominiums in the sketch.

Darn, she had forgotten them. But he needn't think he was going to get off that easily. "The skiing business can be completely unpredictable, you know," she said sweetly. "Maybe you don't really know what you're letting yourself in for. I don't suppose you've had much experience with the reality of running a ski lodge."

The gray eyes were challenging. "And I suppose that you have?"

"Of course," Jennifer said airily. "My father ran Highlands for years. Didn't Darla mention it?"

"Your father—" he said blankly.

"Yes, Nils Ericson, my father. He was the manager here before Claude. He ran Highlands for—oh, ten years. And in some of those years it hardly snowed at all. And other years there was snow up to the rooftops, but there would be a blizzard every weekend to close the roads so nobody could get up the mountain to ski. Other times it would rain on every holiday and no one went skiing. It's not a business you can depend on to make you rich."

"What are you saying?"

She gave him a level stare. "I'm saying, I vote 'no.'"

"What do you mean, no?" His voice was almost a shout.

With a silent apology to Claude and her fingers crossed tightly beneath the sketchbook, Jennifer said with dignity, "I mean that it's too much money; it's too risky. I say that you shouldn't expand Highlands like this. Maybe that's not what you wanted to hear, but you insisted on having my opinion." She closed the sketchbook with a snap. "Now, what are you going to do about it?"

Travis could feel relief coursing through his veins like champagne. This time he had been blessedly wrong. She was no trap, no plant, no snare. She was staring back at him now, challenging and stormy-eyed. Did she know how big a fool he had been? He had a wild urge to confess—to clear the slate—but an uncharacteristic twinge of caution held him back. He had believed before that he could have her—the attraction between them was unmistakable—but now the situation had changed. It was no longer some temporary, take-whatever-you-can-get affair, but something infinitely more important. He felt a little shaken at just how important it had become. He could no longer afford to blunder along like a wild bull, insulting her, walking away from her....

"You haven't answered me," she said.

He had forgotten the question. "I haven't?"

"What are you going to do about this?"

"I don't know what I'm going to do," he said, but it wasn't Highlands he was talking about. He wanted to take her in his arms, make love to her on the spot, right there on the fur rug. A moment ago he would have moved toward her without hesitation, with no thought for the future. Now he wanted her more than ever, but the future was opening up a vista of such dazzling possibilities that he felt the need to hold back, to think carefully about his next move. This was going to be the most important merger of his life!

A tiny frown of puzzlement puckered the perfect line of her brow. She must have sensed the change in him, without understanding in the least the reason for it. How unreasonable he must have seemed to her all this time. What an overbearing idiot he had been....

Jennifer glanced around the room as though his silence were making her uncomfortable.

"It's getting dark," she said, finally.

Outside the windows the world was black. He could plainly see their reflections in the glass, the two of them all gilded and rosy in their own little cocoon of firelight. If he couldn't win her and hold her in this setting, in this isolation, then he deserved to live out his life alone.

"How long were you planning to stay at Highlands?" Travis asked, pursuing this train of thought.

The puzzled line deepened. And then, unexpectedly, a faint blush stained her cheeks. The long lashes came down to veil her eyes. "I don't know... I had no definite plans... it all depended..." She stopped in confusion.

He had the feeling that a curtain had lifted briefly, disclosing some mystery behind the words, one that he hadn't suspected existed. A few minutes ago he would have jumped to the conclusion that the length of her stay depended on himself. Now that he was through with jumping to conclusions, it was clear that there was more to it than that. Something else would determine whether she stayed or left.

Her head came up and the sapphire eyes sparkled. "I'm staying until I get my car back," she said spunkily.

Travis almost blurted out his readiness to buy her a dozen cars. Instead, he managed a look of thoughtful consideration. "We'll have to have someone out to look it over. Weather permitting, of course," he added, giving her a tentative smile.

"Weather permitting," Jennifer repeated, answering his smile with a small one of her own. "How long do you think this storm will go on?"

"Oh, it can't last *too* long," he said with complete honesty. Right now no length of time would be too long for him. It could go on indefinitely, as far as he was concerned.

"Let's hope that the food holds out."

"Well, there seems to be plenty of frozen trout." He didn't want to talk about food. And he particularly didn't want to see her getting to her feet as she was now, and walking away from the firelight—away from him.

The leaping flames crackled vigorously on the hearth, but all the brightness and warmth in the room seemed to drain away when she was no longer there. Without conscious thought, he got up and followed her into the kitchen.

Chapter Eleven

Jennifer stood in front of the kitchen sink and looked with dismay at the heap of thawing trout. She didn't know why she had got up and walked away, leaving the swashbuckling cavalier of her imagination alone. Alone in that little golden oasis where the rest of the world seemed faraway, where the fact that the two of them were there together was the only tangible reality left. It didn't ease the hollow feeling inside her to know that she had felt his eyes follow her as she went. Or that his gaze had been as strong as a touch, as palpable as a caress.

Something was happening to her; she didn't understand what it was. She didn't understand anything—not herself, not him. She knew only that the gloom wrapping itself around her here in the kitchen had nothing to do with the fading of the day, with the darkness outside. It had everything to do with an emptiness inside herself—an emptiness that had seized her without warning and that now was just as suddenly dispelled by the almost inaudible whisper of his approaching footsteps behind her. An almost trancelike cessation of thought took its place.

Silently he stood behind her, his presence as strong as a scream and as impossible to ignore. She closed her eyes and simply waited, feeling her flesh tingle at his nearness, her whole being focused on nothing but the reality of the moment.

Unaware of what she was doing, Jennifer turned to face him, moving slowly, as though walking underwater. For half an eternity—or twenty heartbeats—they stood, inches apart, the current between them surging higher and stronger.

Mutely Travis held out his arms. One dreamlike step brought her into their circle. She leaned her head against his shoulder, her body quickening to his warmth, to his dizzying masculine strength.

The air around them seemed to hum, a note that vibrated too deep for ears to hear, down on the level where their skin and nerve endings responded in a harmony of abandon.

After another eternity, he bent his head toward her. She felt his cheek against hers, his breath on her hair. Still in her trance, she turned her face until their lips met in a kiss that seemed as inevitable as the turning of the earth. Deep within her, slumbering passion awoke. Her bones melted, every inch of her skin came alive.

He kissed her throat, the bared shoulder, the tender hollow over her collarbone. She pressed her hands flat against the muscles of his back as she clung to him, trembling.

At last their passionate embrace slackened. Wordlessly, they turned toward the doorway, moving as one. It was as though he had no more will than she. At the foot of the stairs he made a movement toward her that she interpreted as an intention of sweeping her into his arms to carry her. Somehow that did not coincide with her mood of the moment, and she captured one of his hands instead, holding it tightly in hers. He put his free arm around her waist and pulled her tightly against him while he kissed her once more, a harder, more demanding kiss this time. Then they went upstairs, hand in hand, like children eager to go to bed.

The hallway was quite dark by now, but Travis had left a small lamp burning on the table beside the telephone, so the bedroom was softly lighted. He lifted one questioning eyebrow in that direction, asking without words if she wanted him to turn it off. Jennifer shook her head. Neither of them dared to speak; words would have broken the spell. He released her hand to fling back the bedcovers. She stepped out of her slippers.

Moving unhurriedly now, his hands went to her waist again, this time underneath the loose sweater. Slowly, sensuously, they moved upward on her bare back, burning against the skin. He swept them lightly forward across her breasts and she caught her breath, arching her back in sudden pleasure. He did not pause but deftly lifted the sweater from her body and left her bare to the waist.

The silver-gray eyes widened in appreciation of the perfect shallow cups of her breasts. She fumbled with shaky fingers to unfasten her jeans. He drew her down on the bed and slid his hand along the smooth silky curve of her hip. Jennifer lifted and turned herself against his hands, eager to be free of the confining clothes.

When she was left wearing only a triangular scrap of white satin, Travis drew back momentarily, letting his eyes feast on her. For a moment she lay back against the pillows, accepting his homage, then knelt on the bed in front of him and reached out to unbutton his shirt. Every inch of her skin that had felt his touch was tingling with pleasure, avid for more.

He allowed her to slide the shirt down off his broad shoulders and drop it in a heap on the floor, then caught her to him and stretched her out on the bed again. Keeping one arm around her, he shed the rest of his clothes. He kissed her deeply, his hand slowly stroking her shoulders, her breasts, awakening totally new feelings within her, new fires that burned at the very core of her being.

Gently he kissed her breasts and nipples, taking each of her nipples in turn between his lips, caressing them with his tongue. Each movement sent little currents of pleasure through her, each touch of his hand, each gentle tantalizing caress trailed fingers of fire across her welcoming skin. At last his hand traced the outline of her bikini panties and whispered briefly across the satin triangle, arousing her still further until she was eager, eager and grateful to have him seize the elastic band and strip them away.

Jennifer's breathing quickened as his hand continued to caress and probe, and she grasped his upper arms, digging her fingers deeply into his firm muscular flesh. Entering her gently, Travis stopped at her gasp, but she clutched him harder, drawing him down, down into the throbbing center of her body. He began to move inside her then, slowly, building up her need and his own. She had thought that she couldn't possibly desire him more fiercely, yet now he began to drive her from peak to peak, ever higher and stronger, to a final explosion of passion that at last left her gasping, exhilarated and spent.

"So that's what it's like," she said musingly, as he lay relaxed beside her. She saw him open one eye and look in her direction, but she was talking more to herself than to him.

These had been the strangest two days of her entire life, she thought. It was like being in some twilight zone of the emotions, where inexplicable things kept happening. First there had been the unexpected fiasco with Claude, and now this—this adventure. She must be still in shock. Presumably she would eventually get over it. She'd wake up one day and everything would be back to normal. It was saddening to realize that normality would mean no more Travis in her life, but right now she couldn't make herself feel sad at all, or indeed anything else except wonderful.

"What are you smiling at?" he asked.

Jennifer stretched slowly, luxuriously, and turned dancing sapphire eyes upon him. "Don't you leave all your women smiling?"

He stared, then grinned. "Not always. The saucy ones get spanked."

"How interesting," she said. How incredible! would be more like it. How could she lie here naked beside a naked stranger and exchange light banter! Of course, he was the most beautiful, dashing and adorable stranger she had ever met. And the strangest, too. He had matched her latest mood so perfectly that it was possible to wonder if he were suffering from shock himself. On the other hand, the past two days had shown him to be a creature of innumerable moods—every one of them impossible to predict or explain.

She stretched again, like a lazy cat. She felt as though she'd just had a powerful dream and was now awakening to a most delightful reality. The two of them must have been under the influence of the same spell to have come this far without a word spoken between them, as if some enchanter had sprinkled magic dust over both of them and the effect had not yet worn off. The way it had happened it had to be magic.

Travis propped himself on one elbow and looked down at her. "Now that's a real Mona Lisa smile. What are you thinking about?"

"Fish," she said.

"And what is there about fish that can make you look like that?"

Jennifer looked at him from beneath half-lowered eyelids. "Instead of kissing me in front of the romantic fireplace, you first kissed me in the kitchen in front of the fish."

"You know, you're right. Shall we go back downstairs and see if it works the same way every time?"

Her laughter was sweeter than music to him. Where had this lovely lighthearted creature sprung from? he wondered. All this time he had found her gorgeous, provocative, enthralling—a rich tapestry of enticements, but not one lightened with the brighter colors of gaiety and wit. Now it seemed that she might be not only his dearest love but a heck of a lot of fun as well. It was like finally collaring an aloof and regal tigress, only to find he had also acquired a playful and affectionate kitten. He felt incredibly lucky. It was possible that the joyousness had been there all the time, that his own wrongheaded actions had been suppressing it. He had been an idiot. But he didn't need to be an idiot anymore.

Travis said, "There is at least one more reason to explain your lying there smiling mysteriously at the thought of fish." He was still smiling himself—in fact, he suspected that he couldn't have stopped smiling if he'd tried.

Answering glints of merriment danced in her eyes again. "And what is that?"

"Hunger."

"You can't mean that we should actually eat our magic trout!"

"Plenty more in the freezer where those came from," he pointed out. "Plenty more kisses, too." He leaned over to demonstrate....

They ate their dinner at a small round table that Travis placed in front of the fireplace.

As she set two places with the finest china and crystal, Jennifer wore his white terry cloth bathrobe. It felt like an extension of his arms around her. She even found a vase for a pink silk rosebud that she'd picked from an arrangement of artificial flowers in Darla's room. And just before the trout were ready to be taken out of the broiler, she whisked upstairs and came down again wearing the blue and silver silken robe that floated around her like moonlight.

The trout were unavoidably dry after spending three months in the freezer, and the frozen oriental vegetables were something less than gourmet. Still, the candlelight cast a soft glow over the scene, a glow that the vintage wine complemented from within. Not that either of them paid much attention to what they ate or drank anyway, Jennifer realized. They were too wrapped up in the magic of the moment, in this new awareness of each other.

For dessert she brought out the last cheesecake from the freezer. But even covered with huckleberries and borne in on a metal tray, it somehow failed to measure up to the occasion. Surely the moment called for something special—fireworks, a mammoth cake, a marching band—!

Travis looked at the unprepossessing little mound in the center of the tray. They exchanged glances. Seemingly reading her thoughts, he snapped his fingers. "I know what this needs!" Crossing to the liquor cabinet, he reached for a bottle of fine old brandy. After dousing the cheesecake liberally, he used a long fireplace match to set it aflame.

He stepped back. "There you are! Chef MacKay's world-famous huckleberry cheesecake flambé!" He served the dessert with a flourish. "Perhaps I should patent this and hire an advertising agency to work at putting Cheesecake MacKay on every table in America. Or franchise it. Can't you see the crowds flocking to Cheesecake Chalets all over the country?"

Jennifer shook her head in mock sadness. "It would never work. Cheesecake has a very sinister reputation."

"It has?"

"Everybody thinks of it as being terribly fattening, I'm afraid. Perhaps we'd better keep it as our own secret recipe."

He took a cautious bite. "Perhaps you're right. And I can think of better uses for this particular brandy, too."

When they'd finished eating, he brought out fragile balloon glasses and poured them each a generous after-dinner brandy. Raising his glass to her, he toasted her with his eyes. The moment was so perfect that Jennifer felt her eyelids prickle hotly with sudden unbidden tears. It was wonderful, but it could not last. She tried to blink the tears back. One escaped, just one, and she quickly turned her head toward the hearth. She put her hand up with all the casualness she could muster, touching a fingertip to the wet track on her cheek. She gazed around the firelit room with longing and a touch of resignation.

When she could trust herself to speak, she said, "This is so beautiful. Such a wonderful memory to look back on...."

"What do you mean?" Travis slid his hand forward to cover hers.

Jennifer lowered her eyes. "You know... afterward..."

"After what?"

"After it's over!" she said with a rush.

Chapter Twelve

Jennifer looked up at Travis, encountering the full force of those silver eyes. There was surprise in them—and something else. She wasn't certain what it was—anger, coldness, reserve?

Her heart sank. She never should have blurted out her straying thoughts. Now he was withdrawing his hand from where it rested on hers, now replenishing his glass, studying the deep-ruby color of the vintage brandy. What had she done? Where was the dear laughing playmate of a few minutes ago? Had she summoned that unpredictable anger that seemed always so ready to erupt?

The gray gaze that swept up briefly to meet her own before it settled moodily on the leaping fire had no warmth in it, just a blankness, a wary coolness she had not seen in him before.

For a moment Jennifer was bewildered. Then her whirling thoughts seized on a possible explanation. A rich and eligible bachelor would naturally encounter more than enough young women who were eager to marry him for his money alone. Her unthinking remark could easily have been interpreted as a plea for permanence, a demand for a marriage proposal. No wonder he was looking thoughtful.

At least he hadn't gone storming up the stairs again; that was something. She had a chance to make good her blunder—if she could only think of a way to do it. She pictured herself putting her hand on his arm, saying, "Don't worry, I know this isn't real. It's too beautiful and too sudden—too perfect to be real. One moment soon the magic will disappear and we'll look around us with our ordinary sane, sensible eyes, and we'll be just pleasant strangers." Something cried out inside her at that prospect, but she kept her tears under control. Although it surely had to end, *oh, please, don't let it end right now,* her heart was saying.

"I just meant," she said, almost too brightly, "that this storm is going to be over sometime. Nobody gets to stay in ShangriLa forever."

Travis came back then from whatever far place his attention had strayed to. The eyes that met hers were clear and alive. "Bite your tongue," he said. And smiled.

Relief flooded her. "It's the truth," she insisted, a little giddily. "One of these days the world is going to come tramping through the trees and search us out. Whether we want it to or not."

"We'll hide," he said, his eyes dancing.

"I've always heard that you can run, but you can't hide. The telephone company will get you if no one else does. You may think you're safe but just wait. One of these days they'll find you again, and the first thing you know they'll have you back on long distance to Kansas City."

"That's not a pretty picture," Travis said, not entirely in fun. Surprisingly, the life that had felt so completely rich and full to him only a few hours ago now seemed flat and sadly lacking. And what it lacked was sitting across the table from him, giving the room and everything in it a reason for being.

All the usual warning signals had hoisted themselves in his mind when she'd begun to talk of "memories" and "afterward." Woman Angling for Marriage Proposal flashed in neon lights in his head. Danger: Commitment Ahead blared the warning bells. His well-honed bachelor reflexes had sealed his lips and set him studying the fire before any incautious word could escape. Suddenly he had thought: What am I doing? I was ready to give myself up to this woman when I believed unspeakable things about her. And now here she is, her own dear, desirable self, and I react as though she just tried to pick my pocket because she mentions "afterward."

He said, "The long-distance telephone can be a hard taskmaster. Can you imagine sharing your life with one of them?" he added, putting out a tentative feeler of his own.

"I'm afraid that high finance will always be a deep dark mystery to me," Jennifer replied. "I'll settle for sleepy-eyed lions any time."

"Lions?" he said blankly.

She put her hands up in front of her face and mimed snapping a picture. "It's what I do for a living. I'm a photographer."

"Of lions?" He felt totally disconcerted, as though he had missed the last step on a dark stairway.

"Didn't you know? No? Well, I suppose that Darla just never got around to mentioning it."

"That you photograph lions?" Travis knew he must sound like a stuck phonograph record, but somehow he couldn't seem to assimilate that astounding bit of information.

"Only once. The lions, I mean. And they were extremely sleepy-eyed. It wasn't a roaring success." She paused expectantly, and he realized that she expected him to laugh. He managed a smile and motioned for her to continue.

It was her turn to look perplexed. "I guess I just expected that you knew all of this. Maybe I pictured you pumping Darla for all the details of the strange female that fate had dropped into your hot tub."

No, he hadn't asked questions. Because he'd thought that he already knew all the answers. But he couldn't tell her that. That would have to be his secret.

It was sobering to realize that he knew almost nothing at all about her. At least that was an oversight that he could easily remedy.

"Tell me about yourself," Travis said. "Where have you been all these years since you left Highlands? And what brought you back here at last?"

Now it was Jennifer's turn to fall silent. "It's a long story and a boring one," she said finally.

"We're not exactly pressed for time," he said genially. "How about giving me a few of the highlights? I promise not to go to sleep."

"You should be careful about making rash promises you might not be able to keep," she teased, trying to keep the evening's playfulness alive. But her heart obviously wasn't in it. Something was troubling her, and he listened with sharpened attention as she told him briefly about her life since leaving Highlands.

He became still and alert at the first mention of Brian but relaxed as her recital continued. Plainly, there was no emotional entanglement there.

"Do you regret giving up your modeling career?" he asked, when she had finished.

"No, not at all." She added, slowly, "At first it seemed quite...thrilling...for a year or two." She searched for the words to explain her feelings. "And then...I don't know why...somehow it just wasn't the same. It wasn't enough—just standing there having my picture taken."

He nodded. It made perfect sense to him that she would prefer to be up and doing, using her own talents, taking charge of her life.

"And what about the photography?" he said. "Do you think that is what you want to do?"

"Oh, yes," she said simply. "I'm still developing my technical skill, but I have confidence in my own eye, my own way of looking at things."

Travis approved of that, too. Find what you're good at and go for it. That was a motto he could endorse. He felt that he had opened up an enlightening new window on Jennifer's life, one that showed her to be a more complex and fascinating creature than he had suspected. He knew her better—and yet in some ways she was no less puzzling than before. There was an elusive something—almost a sadness in her, still to be accounted for.

"So you've been away in Texas—and other places—for all these years," he said musingly as she fell silent again. "And this is the first time you've been back to Highlands." That in itself was rather strange. He could understand her mother's reluctance to return to the place where her husband had died, but Jennifer seemed to regard Highlands mainly with nostalgic affection. "But I expect you kept in touch with Claude through the years," he added as an afterthought.

The dark lashes swept down to veil her eyes. "No, I didn't. Not at all." She stood up and began to stack the dishes with unsteady hands.

Now why should Claude's name have that effect on her? Perhaps she resented him for taking her father's place. But no, it couldn't be that. She hadn't said much to Claude over the telephone, but there had been no animosity in her voice or attitude. And he had certainly been straining every muscle to catch and analyze the faintest nuance of their exchange, because that was when he'd still believed that the two of them were plotting together. That seemed a really paranoid idea now, and he was suitably ashamed of it. But it still left the unanswered riddle of why a simple question about Claude should make her hands begin to tremble.

Jennifer avoided his eyes and turned away. As she left the room, he picked up the metal tray, now slightly the worse for wear after his experiment in cookery. He carried it out to the kitchen and set it down next to where she was rinsing the plates.

"Come away from there," he said, so commandingly that she turned to look at him in surprise.

"That robe was never meant to see the inside of a kitchen." Travis slid his arms around her, gently turning her away from the sink. The smoothness of the silk under his hands was like the remembered smoothness of her skin. Through the semisheer material he could glimpse the thin spaghetti straps of a matching gown, a mere wisp of the same blue and silver silk. "Don't tell me that you're in the habit of washing dishes in this little outfit."

Jennifer looked down in some confusion, still with that faintly startled look that widened her eyes, making her at the same time more tempting and more vulnerable.

"You're right," she said. "I—I didn't think of that. It's just—I've never worn this before."

His arms tightened around her, meeting with no resistance as she surrendered to his embrace. All of his senses responded to her closeness as he buried his face in the clean fragrance of her hair. But his analytical mind would not be still. He knew expensive clothes when he saw them, and the price of this gown and robe must have been astronomical. And when in her life does a woman spend her money most recklessly on the most beautiful, most sensuous night-wear she can find? The answer came unbidden into his mind with startling clarity. For a first night of love. For her wedding night or for the night she knows she is going to be with a lover.

He could no longer leap to the conclusion that every move she made was part of an elaborate plot calculated to entice him to approve Claude's plans—but one huge unanswered question remained. What lover was waiting for her here?

"You came a long way," he murmured into her ear.

"What?" she said, half drowsily.

"You came a long way from Fort Worth."

"Oh. That's right. Almost two thousand miles," she agreed.

"And you had been away for quite a while," Travis persisted. "What was it that inspired you to come back here just at this particular time?" He tried to keep the words light, undemanding.

She sighed dreamily. "Just luck, I guess," she said. Her body was relaxed trustingly against him, the faint warmth of her flesh tantalizing through the cool of the thin silk. But still he asked the next question, almost in spite of himself.

"But why Highlands? I mean, you don't have a job here, no commission for photographs or anything. It's not as though there are any animals here that you could use—even the Saint Bernards are up at Timberline."

Jennifer stirred in his arms. He waited tensely, expecting any of the dozen excuses that she might reasonably offer: that she was taking a little vacation and just wanted to see the old place, that she had come to photograph ski layouts on speculation, that she was just passing through on her way to somewhere else. So many ordinary explanations could account for her presence here. But there was only one explanation that could account for an expensive new peignoir that floated around her like moonlight.

She didn't answer the question. Travis waited, holding her lightly. After a long, long pause, she said, "It was only silliness."

"What do you mean?"

She straightened, moving back slightly. "Just that it wasn't anything important."

"It must have had some significance at the time, to bring you two thousand miles." He heard the sharp edge to the words and regretted it, but it was too late to call it back.

Jennifer reacted to his tone of voice more than to the words themselves. The impatience, the sudden ring of anger struck her like a cascade of icy water. *It's happening again,* she thought. That sudden, total, utter unreasonableness on his part that always surfaced without warning, without any visible cause.

So this was to be the end of everything. The bubble had burst, the music had stopped. She'd known that it would come, but why did it have to happen so soon? It gave her no pleasure to realize that she had been right all along. These few hours, these magical hours, were as insubstantial and fleeting as she had believed they would be. Somewhere deep inside her there must have been a shy flicker of hope that she would be proven wrong, because there was no placid acceptance in her, only a sudden blazing anger.

"You do it every time! *Every single time!*"

"What are you talking about?" he demanded.

"You know perfectly well what I mean." She stepped back from his embrace.

Travis's hands closed on her forearms, and his strength held her in place. "You're not making any sense."

"*I'm* not making any sense! It's you—you're the one who doesn't make sense." She twisted futilely in his grasp. "And I am sick of it. *Sick of it!* Let me go! You can have this latest tantrum all by yourself. I don't want to see it."

His grip on her tightened. "I'm not the one who's having the tantrum here—"

"Now it's my fault, is it? I should have expected that would be the next thing in your bag of tricks. No wonder Darla was afraid to tell you that she wrecked my car—she knew what kind of reaction to expect from your temper." She stopped struggling and stood straight and tense, her head back challengingly.

"Come on now!" The anger in his voice was displaced by amazement. "Darla's never been afraid of me. You must know that. You only have to be with her about fifteen minutes to realize that she is perfectly capable of twisting everyone she knows around her little finger."

"And that's not right, either. You shouldn't let it be like that. You can't keep letting her get away with doing all these...these heedless things she does. Someday the trouble she gets into will be serious." The words tumbled out beyond her control. "She'll hurt someone—or herself—and it won't be something that Big Brother can fix by throwing money at it!"

Travis gave her a little shake. "You're not making sense!" he repeated.

"I'm making perfect sense," Jennifer responded with dignity. "And whether I make sense or not is no concern of yours, anyway. What I say or do is my business, and I don't need your approval or your endorsement. You just provide me with a car that isn't a wreck and see how fast I get out of here. You can have your house all to yourself. And you can go back to bashing telephones and slamming doors to your heart's content!"

"I haven't bashed any phones or slammed any doors," he said mildly.

"Don't talk to me like I'm some hysterical woman." She was not to be put off by his soothing tones. "*Mentally* you've bashed telephones. *Emotionally* you've slammed doors. And everything else in your path. Including the people."

"What in the world did I do to make you so angry?"

Suddenly she was tired. It was like beating her head against a brick wall. "Does it matter?" she said coldly.

"Of course it matters. I ought to know whatever it is that I am apologizing for."

"Don't bother with any apologies. It's too late, anyway."

"Too late? What are you talking about?" Travis shook her again, his face like a thundercloud. "Will you start making sense, Jennifer!"

So he didn't like it when someone took his own irrational anger and flung it back in his face. Jennifer didn't know how long she could keep it up, but she knew she had to cling tight to that anger, because to let go would be to give in to the flood of tears she could feel pressing behind her eyelids, ready to burst forth the instant her guard was let down.

"I knew it could never last," she said. "But I didn't think you would spoil it so soon."

"What does that mean—you knew it couldn't last?"

"It didn't, did it?" She spoke with such quiet conviction that he loosened his grip on her arms and stepped back a pace. "A few hours," she went on. "That's all we had." She turned away, her head bent, the thick dark curtain of her hair swinging forward like a barrier between them.

Travis didn't recognize the pain in her voice, only the finality. It seemed to be telling him that prior claims had reasserted themselves. She had brought a whispering silken robe to Highlands to wear in the arms of one special man—and that man was not Travis MacKay. The snowstorm had given them this little gift of time, a brief interlude out of the world—but now reality was creeping in. And the reality of this other man was too strong for her to fight.

"Are you saying that it's all over?" he said hoarsely.

Jennifer moved her head in a small, hopeless gesture of assent.

"Well, it isn't over for me, dammit!" he said, and gathered her into his arms.

Chapter Thirteen

For a moment Jennifer was acquiescent, lying against Travis's broad chest in stunned surprise. Then her head came up.

"Okay, Spitfire, let's slug it out," he said, releasing her. "We got off on the wrong foot at the very beginning, and we've had misunderstandings and blowups between us ever since. But we've had something else, too." He took a fold of her wide silk sleeve between his thumb and forefinger. "I want you to know that the man you bought this for is going to have a fight on his hands."

If a brief flame of hope had been born in her heart, it flickered out at his final words. Though she was not now in love with Claude—and perhaps never had been—she didn't feel she could speak his name and turn Travis into his enemy. A powerful and implacable enemy, at that.

"You don't want to tell me who he is," Travis said thoughtfully.

Jennifer stood motionless, wary. Watching him.

"Perhaps I wouldn't need to know who he is—if I were sure of *you*." He took her hand. She hadn't realized how cold her fingers had become until she felt the warmth of his.

Anger and hope had fled together, leaving her drained, calm but sad. She shook her head slowly. "You've convinced yourself that there is another man. I don't think you'll be content until you have his name."

He rubbed his thumb back and forth across her cold palm. "Perhaps not. Maybe that's a question we don't have to deal with right now. Come into the other room and talk—or at least listen to me. Come in by the fire."

Jennifer followed, unresisting, as he led her by the hand. She sank down on the thick fur rug and stared into the flames while he returned the small round table to its place in the corner. When he came back, she stiffened slightly, but he seated himself on the brick hearth, giving her breathing room.

He poked the fire moodily and added more logs, prolonging the silence until the tension was unbearable.

"As I see it," he said at last, "you were upset just now because you believed that I was angry."

"You *were* angry," she said flatly.

For a minute he looked as though he were about to deny it. He rammed the poker into his carefully built fire and the logs fell apart in a shower of sparks. "Suppose I say that I'm sorry?" he offered, without conviction.

"It isn't merely that you get angry at times," Jennifer said, choosing her words carefully. "It's that I never can tell *why* you're angry. Dealing with you is like walking through a world filled with tiger traps—those camouflaged pits in the ground full of sharpened stakes. They look so innocent from above; you think everything is fine. But suddenly—bang—the ground goes out from under your feet."

"And that's what you think I'm like."

"Oh, what's the use of talking about it!" she exclaimed. "You *are* like that."

Travis rearranged the burning logs with the poker. After a long silence, he said, "I mistook you for someone else."

She didn't know what to make of this apparent change of subject. "You did?"

"Yes, I thought you were someone else. When we first met on Widowmaker I thought I knew exactly who you were. Then when you showed up in the hot tub I was sure. All this time I thought I knew."

"Who did you think I was?" Curiosity gave her voice more life.

"Someone I'd been half expecting. Someone imported by Claude. Someone whose job was to be...agreeable."

Her eyes widened in shock. "You mean—you expected Claude to supply you with—with a woman?"

He turned on her so suddenly that she recoiled. "Of course not! But I thought he might *try*. As he has done before. I needed a housekeeper this spring, and presto! he produces a nice domestic blonde who can wash dishes and cook, in between giving me sidelong glances and singing the praises of Highlands as the next St. Moritz. That one was too obvious. The second one was a little more subtle—she decorated this house. She came with Claude's recommendation, too."

Jennifer frowned. "But you can't really be sure—"

His mouth twisted wryly. "You mean that I'm paranoid as well as unstable? No—I won't go into the details, but believe me, I'm sure."

"Were you angry with Claude? Did you tell him so?"

Travis shrugged. "There didn't seem to be any point in making an issue of it. Claude's a Frenchman. He'd do almost anything to make Highlands great. He didn't know that he was hurting his cause instead of furthering it."

Her brow grew furrowed. "Then, all those times you were angry—it was because you thought I was like those other two women?"

"I was angry because I believed that Claude had planted you on me—and I found you irresistible."

"Oh," she said in a small voice. That was something she wasn't ready to deal with right now. Her thoughts fled back to the scene of their first encounter. "Then...right from the very beginning...on the mountain...."

"That's right. I thought you fell down on purpose. A little more realistically than you intended, maybe, but all with the intention of arranging a meeting between us. I wasn't surprised to see you— or someone like you. And things had been going badly all day. When you showed up, I just let you have it with both barrels. It was all a case of mistaken identity."

Jennifer considered his words for a moment. "How can you be sure?"

"Sure of what?"

"That you were wrong about me. I still don't see any proof that I'm not exactly what you thought I was."

"Oh, no. I gave you an opening when I asked for your advice. And you said not to build. Not to take the chance."

She leaned back against the big floor cushion. "Maybe I just took a chance myself. After all, it was perfectly obvious that you were going to go ahead with the project, no matter what anyone said."

Travis looked at her sharply. "What do you mean? How was it obvious?"

"Well—there's all the money you've already spent, for one thing."

He shook his head. "That proves nothing. I could sell the land lease and this house any time. And walk away with a good profit."

"That sketch wasn't drawn by anyone who was thinking of walking away. Your little skier and ice skater had too much personality—there was too much joy in them." She hadn't thought it out in so many words at the time, but now she realized that it was quite true.

He smiled faintly. "You mean that I gave myself away? Most people wouldn't be so perceptive."

"That's my stock-in-trade, the photographer's eye. Anyone can learn the mechanics of using the camera and the darkroom, but a photographer has to be able to look at things a little more clearly than the next person—or at least a little differently. But you made it easy, really. Your feelings for your subjects come through very strongly in your drawings."

"All right, maybe you did see through me," Travis conceded. "You were sure I meant to go ahead with the expansion—and yet you advised me not to do it. So you really think it's a bad idea—a poor risk."

Jennifer shook her head. "I don't know the first thing about the risks. I don't see where all the money will come from. Or all the customers, if you do get it built," she added slowly. "But you're the businessman; you know what you're doing. I'd love to see all those neat things at Highlands—the pool and the gondola and the hotel and everything. But the reason I said no was because—this sounds silly, but you'll know what I mean—because it was plain that you were toying with me. Pretending my opinion really counted when it didn't make the slightest bit of difference." A tinge of anger crept into her voice. "So there you are. Just when you thought it was safe to be nice to me...to go to bed with me..." She faltered, then her voice grew stronger. "You find that you can't be sure of me after all. Maybe your worst fears are true. Maybe I *am* all the awful things you believed I was.''

''No, you're not.'' He ran his fingers through his thick shock of black hair, leaving it endearingly rumpled. ''In spite of all the evidence, I'm sure that you're not.''

Jennifer stiffened. ''In spite of all *what* evidence?'' she demanded hotly.

Travis looked startled, then defensive. ''Well, there just didn't seem to be any other explanation that would account for your sudden presence out there on the mountain, sprawled across my path like that. You weren't a member of the general public—the lodge wasn't open to the public yet. And you were no employee—I made some inquiries inside and found out that much. So who were you? No one knew.''

''You might have asked *me*.''

''When? In the hot tub? I suppose I could have stood there with my bare legs hanging out in the cold and said, 'Pardon me, are you a lady of easy virtue hired to tempt me with your body, or are you merely a beautiful young innocent whom fate had somehow deposited in my hot tub with no clothes on?' ''

His rueful smile took some of the sting out of his words, but she felt the hot blood rise to her cheeks at the memory. ''Too bad you didn't say it,'' she said. ''We might have had all this out in the open twenty-four hours ago.'' Then she thought it over and shook her head. "Maybe even that wouldn't have helped. Last night I just assumed that you must be drunk."

"So you rose up from the water like Venus rising from the sea. And snatched my bathrobe and left me there, exposed to the elements." He smiled with reminiscent pleasure. "Someday, before we grow old and gray together, you'll have to tell me how you managed to get yourself marooned out there without a stitch of clothing anywhere in sight."

"Since there's no chance of us ever growing old together, I'll tell you right now," Jennifer replied. "It only takes one word—Darla."

Travis nodded. "I can believe that she had a hand in it. I just can't picture how it came about."

She had a suspicion that he was laughing at her, but she couldn't pass up the opportunity to set the record straight. "It was Darla who decided it was unnecessary to carry in my heavy suitcases and dig out a bathing suit—because we were absolutely and positively all alone here, without another house or person for miles. Then she managed to knock my robe into the tub, and she took it inside when she went to find me something else to wear."

"That sounds like a typical Darla happening."

She shook her head. "Thoughtlessness I can understand. And I can see that that might be typical. But I never would have believed that she was the kind to do something intentionally malicious—like sending you out there while I was in—in—"

"In such an exposed position?" he supplied helpfully. "Well, you don't need to blame her. I can account for that. She thought I was safely upstairs on the telephone while she concocted something special for me to drink out of the bartender's guide. But once she'd mentioned that the girl with the gorgeous eyes was out in my hot tub, I decided that the two of us should have a little confrontation of our own. And what do you mean there's no chance of us growing old together?"

The abrupt change of subject caught her unprepared. For a minute her thoughts scurried in every direction. "Let's—let's stick to the original subject," she managed to stammer.

"I'd rather talk about us."

"Well, I wouldn't." She rallied. "Just what other 'evidence' did you feel you had against me?"

"Evidence?" Now Travis seemed to be the one who had to marshal his scattered thoughts. "Oh. Well, there was the phone call from Claude. I was standing there looking into your eyes, forgetting that Claude's little plots had ever existed. Then the telephone rang, and he said something about everything being under control, and it all came crashing down around my ears again."

"I see." Jennifer closed her eyes, remembering each encounter. Knowing that it hadn't been his anger that had upset her so much as the unreasonableness of it. Now that she could look at events from his point of view, they did somehow make sense. Except for one thing.

"I just don't see any evidence that speaks in my favor," she said. "So it looks like any sensible person would still be convinced that I am guilty as charged."

He left his seat on the hearth and moved down onto the rug beside her, so close that they were almost touching. "You may think that I am unbeatable in the role of prosecuting attorney, but just wait until you see me as Perry Mason for the defense." Almost absentmindedly he picked up her hand. But there was nothing casual about the electric thrill that went through Jennifer at his touch.

He said, "The boy behind the counter at the lodge didn't know you, which he certainly would have done if you were an employee there. But he's just a kid, and Nils Ericson was before his time. And so was his beautiful daughter, Jennifer. But the older employees would definitely remember you. And they would no doubt fall all over themselves to provide you with rental skis and chair lift rides and anything else your heart desired. *That* would account for your presence on the ski slope. And, as you pointed out to me at the time, anyone can take a fall. So that demolishes the first count against you.''

Travis put her hand gently against his cheek and half closed his eyes. The warmth of his skin seemed to blaze against her fingers and palm. She could scarcely follow his words as he went on.

''The whole hot tub farce was engineered by Darla—quite unintentionally, of course. So that only leaves Claude's telephone message, which was merely a reassurance about the coming storm from an old friend. There,'' he said triumphantly, ''the court dismisses the case. And apologizes to the defendant for ever doubting her for even one instant.''

Jennifer tried to take her hand away. His grip tightened, held firm. The movement and her body's heightened sensitivity made her freshly aware of the cool sensuous slide of silk against her skin. Her consciousness of the robe that she had bought to wear in the arms of another man served to recall her to reality. Travis had disposed of every question standing between them—except for the most important one of all. Now he would be waiting to hear the name of the man who had drawn her back to Highlands after all these years.

Chapter Fourteen

Now that he had made his confession and cleared up all the misunderstandings between them, now that it was all off his chest, Travis felt relief, happiness, excitement. A wave of desire engulfed him, and he pictured himself pressing his lips to the cool softness of Jennifer's fingertips, the slender fragility of her wrist. At that moment he could have rained kisses on her arm and shoulder as extravagantly as any silent screen lover.

What stopped him was the tension he felt in the hand he was holding. The fingers were rigid and cold against his cheek. When he looked into her face, her eyes were great pools of unhappiness. Something told him to proceed slowly and with the utmost care, because a wrong step now might be disastrous.

He lowered her hand, covering it with both of his own. As they faced each other, motionless, time seemed to tick on endlessly, isolating the two of them in their little circle of firelight.

There was a long, strained silence. Finally he said, "Listen!"

Jennifer stirred. A log in the grate popped softly. Otherwise everything was still.

"I don't hear anything."

"That's just it," he said. "The wind must have dropped. The worst of the storm is over."

Travis got to his feet, maintaining his hold on her hand, so that she had to come with him. "Let's have a look," he said, trying to keep his voice nonchalant.

The large room was in semidarkness, lit only by the glow of the fire. By pressing close to the windows, they could see outside to where fat snowflakes were falling straight down, no longer drifting before the insistent wind. Even though the snow was coming down as thick and fast as ever, it was plain that the storm that held the two of them imprisoned was starting to lose its power. It no longer seemed as though endless hours stretched before them. The stillness marked the beginning of the end of this bittersweet interlude, and if there was to be a future for them beyond this time, Travis knew he had to utilize every minute.

He had a sudden inspiration.

"What a perfect night for hot tubbing!" he said with genuine enthusiasm.

"In this?" Jennifer gestured toward the falling snow with her free hand.

"Trust me. If you can't have a starry night, this is the next best thing."

She stepped back a pace. He freed her hand, making it look like something done almost absent-mindedly, taking the opportunity to release her from any actual physical restraint she might be feeling at his touch.

She said, "That snowdrift between the tub and the back door is probably waist-high by now. You'd have to shovel your way through."

He raised both arms and struck an exaggerated muscle-man pose, tensing them to make his biceps bulge. "Just watch the snow fly once I get started."

Jennifer laughed a little, which was what he had been angling for. Then she shook her head. "How could you get the water hot enough in weather like this?"

"Lady, that heater was *made* for weather like this."

"But—it would take forever." She continued to find reasons why it couldn't be done.

"The evening is still young," he said lightly. "And correct me if I'm wrong, but I don't think either of us has any appointments to keep. We're not going anyplace. Except for me, of course—I'm on my way to find a shovel."

Jennifer stayed by the fire until she heard the door to the deck close behind him. Some of the emotional charge seemed to go out of the air around her then. Now that she was alone, she felt that she could breathe more easily. She recognized his snow-shoveling ploy for what it was—an attempt to ease the tension that had built up between the two of them. She was truly grateful for the respite, however impractical his hot tubbing idea must surely prove to be. He couldn't be expecting her to—oh, no, not possibly! There was no way; her mind simply refused to think of it.

Her mind did acknowledge that this was her golden opportunity to get out of the peignoir and into something altogether less sexy and provocative. She should never have put it on. That had been a tragic mistake, a disaster in every way. It had only raised questions in his mind to which she could supply no answers.

She made her way up the stairs, treading softly as though he might hear her flight and interrupt his labors to order her back again. It bolstered her confidence to be back in her jeans and boots, although there was nothing to wear with them except for Darla's revealing sweater. If she could have found a safety pin she would have closed the neckline primly around her throat. She felt that she needed all the cover she could get.

She thought of her suitcases in the trunk of Darla's Porsche, resting somewhere in a ditch beside the road and probably buried beneath three feet of snow by now. How she wished she had those clothes here. The long-sleeved, high-collared shirt, the bulky knit sweater, the wool après-ski skirt that covered her to her ankles—they were the things she needed now.

Standing in the center of her bedroom, holding the loose neckline closed with one hand, Jennifer could feel the thudding beat of her frightened heart. This apprehension, this near-panic, was something new to her. What was she afraid of? Of Travis? Or the cruelty of love? Fickle, will-o'-the-wisp, never-to-be-trusted love.

She sat down in an upholstered chair by the windows and made herself take several deep breaths. She tried to think more rationally. All right now, she told herself, just what is the matter with me, anyway? Suddenly I feel frightened, and I don't know why. She breathed deeply again, and felt her racing pulse begin to slow down.

Am I afraid of Travis? she asked herself. Afraid he might try to make love to me again? Afraid that he won't? No, she decided, it wasn't that. But there had been something different about him, a change in attitude after all that talk about evidence and misunderstandings. It was as though he had thrown off a burden, or—a checkrein—something that had been holding him back. And now that that something was gone, she sensed that he was ready to move boldly forward into a new phase of their relationship, one where promises and commitments might be given— and demanded.

Heaven help her, she hadn't come to terms with the old entanglements yet! Oh, she had definitely dragged herself out of the little cocoon of illusions she'd been encased in for all these past years. But she was hardly ready to unfurl butterfly wings and go skimming off into the sunshine. Not yet. If she did have any wings, she felt they must be sad and crumpled ones—poor little things that needed time to stretch and grow and learn what flying was all about.

And time was one luxury that was being denied her. There hadn't been a tranquil minute, literally not one since the two big shocks—of finding that love had somehow turned into a dead infatuation and seeing her new little car being turned into a pile of junk.

And that wasn't all. In fact, that was merely the beginning. This afternoon had brought another unsettling experience—that magical time when she and Travis had moved together like two dancers compelled by the rhythms of some irresistible music. Those were the kind of rare moments that should be savored slowly, treasured up in her heart to be dreamed on.

But there was no time, no time at all. Jennifer felt as if she were being bundled along willy-nilly, harried and hurried from one roller coaster swoop to another. There seemed to be no letup. This little section of the world was not about to stop for one minute to let her get off. That was a fact made all the more evident by the slam of a door down below and the stamp of booted feet in the hall. Now she had to take herself down there to meet him, because if she stayed where she was, he would surely be right up here looking for her.

When she started down the stairs, the hallway was empty, but footprints of melting snow on the carpet marked his passage. Jennifer checked an instinctive urge to hurry down and clean them up before the moisture soaked into the material. It would never do to start acting as though this were *her* house. That was one mistake she did not intend to make.

She paused on the bottom step as Travis came out of the kitchen, having shed his parka and boots.

"And who is it that takes care of the carpets in your house in town?" she inquired, as lightly as she could manage. "I'm assuming that you do have one, somewhere."

"In San Francisco," he responded briefly, glancing at the marks on the carpet with no sign of concern or guilt. "That's nothing but nice clean snow. But I know what you're thinking—and you're right. I always wipe my feet before walking on Mrs. Reilly's floors. She's been our live-in housekeeper for so many years that she thinks the place is hers."

"All eighty rooms of it, I suppose?" she suggested, using the same bantering tone to cover up the fact that she was getting that breathless feeling again, standing here so close to him.

"Oh, it's just your average little Nob Hill mansion," he said, glowing with exercise and high spirits. "Who knows how many rooms it might have? Who bothers to count?"

The height of the step brought her almost to his height—her eyes looked directly into his gray ones, into his clear, laughing, dark-fringed eyes.

And those surprisingly light eyes lazily looked her up and down, surveying her from neck to ankles and back again, lingering longest at her right shoulder, where Darla's sweater exposed bare skin. She braced herself for questions about why she had changed her clothes, but he merely said, "I expect the fire needs building up again by now."

He switched off the hall light as he turned in that direction, apparently taking for granted that she would follow where he led.

The fire had subsided into a heap of glowing red coals where an occasional small blue flame flickered briefly before vanishing. The heavy furniture in the room loomed as dimly-glimpsed shapes in the semi-darkness. Travis skillfully arranged fresh wood on the coals, and the room brightened as flames began to lick along the underside of the logs.

Jennifer stood back, watching him, intrigued by the play of light and shadow that filled the room with warm color and silhouetted his strong well-knit body in bold relief against the leaping flames. She sighed.

"What is it?" he said alertly.

"I was just wishing that I had a camera here."

He glanced around the room appraisingly. "Wouldn't it be a little tricky, taking pictures in this light?"

"It would be a challenge," she agreed, "but worth the effort."

After a moment he said, "I guess Darla has a lot to answer for."

"That's the understatement of the year," Jennifer observed, striving to keep her tone light. She moved forward and sank down gracefully onto the big floor cushion in front of the hearth. His sketch-book was lying on the rug where it had been discarded earlier. She picked it up and leafed through it idly, glad of the distraction.

Travis was still studying the problem of capturing the scene without a camera. "A sketch would be no good here," he decided. "Black and white just won't do it. It has to be color—or nothing."

She nodded agreement. She came to the sketch of Darla, and stopped turning pages. He leaned forward to see what had caught her attention.

She held the book up so he could see. "When did you do this?"

"Last summer sometime. Late last summer."

"That recently?" She was surprised.

"Yes," he said, his voice puzzled. "Why do you ask?"

"Is this the way you see her now?"

"I believe it's a pretty fair likeness," he said, in carefully neutral tones.

"It's an excellent likeness," she agreed. "But it isn't Darla."

He took the sketchbook from her hand and frowned down at the page. "It certainly looks like Darla to me."

"Then you're seeing her still as a young dewy-eyed child. The kind you indulge with shiny red toys. And she is, what? Nearly nineteen? Darla's a young adult now—or she should be."

Without moving at all, he seemed to draw away from her. "I think we've had this conversation before," he said coldly.

"You're right." How had she blundered her way into this argument once more? she wondered miserably. "I never meant to bring it up again. I'm sorry."

After a few brooding moments of staring at the picture, Travis said, "You're saying that I've done a lousy job of bringing up my little sister."

"I'm not saying that at all. I like her very much. She's good-hearted, even lovable—"

"Well, then?" he asked, challengingly.

"I'm just saying that she behaves very irresponsibly—and I expect that you encourage her to act that way."

"*Me?* How am I supposed to be doing that?"

Jennifer stiffened, straightening her back. "She does things like not telling you about the accident—running off with my clothes and cameras. That Porsche seems to be part and parcel of most of these problems. She drove it this morning after promising not to. She had the accident because she was having fun driving too fast and tooting the horn. Does it really seem right to you to make her a present of a high-performance sports car? And bright red, at that."

"Does your famous photographer's eye tell you that bright red is an irresponsible color, then?" he inquired with heavy sarcasm.

"It can be, in a way." She spoke slowly now, more gently than before. "Perhaps you had to take on too much responsibility too young—raising Darla, making money. And you unconsciously encourage her to be reckless and free—"

Travis cut her off in midsentence. "Let's do without the amateur psychiatry."

She saw that she had hurt him, and she hadn't set out to do that at all. "I'm sorry," she said again. "I know it's none of my business."

He didn't answer, only turned to stare into the flames. Jennifer followed his lead, thinking how handy it was to have a fire as a focus for attention when you didn't want to look at another person. The silence stretched unbroken. The flicker of the firelight exerted its almost-hypnotic influence, banishing thought, soothing turbulent emotions.

She was deep in reverie when he spoke again. "Let's not fight," he said mildly. "This storm may be over soon," he added without further comment, though both of them knew he was saying that it was these moments alone together that would soon be finished.

She was shocked at the pang that went through her at the thought.

"The water in the hot tub will soon be hot," he said.

Oh, dear, she had the feeling that the roller coaster was clacking up the incline, getting ready for another big swoop. "I'm not sure that's such a good idea," she said faintly.

"Trust me," he said, flashing her a sudden grin that looked anything but trustworthy.

"I still haven't any bathing suit to wear," she pointed out.

"Hmm," he said thoughtfully. "Would you believe me if I promised not to look?"

"Should I?"

"Not for a minute. Believing it would insult my masculinity."

"Well, I certainly wouldn't want to do *that*." Jennifer smiled faintly. "So we're right back where we started."

"I'll tell you what. If the guest has to go without—the host will go without, too. For hospitality's sake. Don't thank me, it's the least I can do."

"I wouldn't dream of imposing on your generosity." Then, more soberly, she suggested, "Don't you think it would be better all around if we stayed out of that hot tub? Wouldn't it make things less... complicated?"

Travis slid onto the big cushion beside her, his arm around her waist, his face against her hair. "If we climb in or stay out, it won't make the slightest bit of difference. Our fate is sealed."

"Can you really believe that?" she said.

"Can you believe I love you?"

"Can I—?" Words failed her.

His embrace tightened. "Because I do, you know."

A paralysis of surprise held her motionless, speechless for a moment. Then common sense came to her rescue. "You can't fall in love in twenty-four hours," she said positively.

"Sure you can. You can fall in love in twenty-four *seconds*. I think that's just about how long it took me to do it. One long, long look into those beautiful blue eyes, and I was a goner."

"I'm talking *seriously*!" she protested.

"You think I'm not? Anyway, it's more than twenty-four hours. Let's see, it must be at least thirty hours by now. Thirty hours since the lightning struck—"

"Don't joke," she warned him. "I mean what I'm saying. One day is not enough!"

"But don't you think this has been a very concentrated kind of courtship, being thrown together like this? One of our hours ought to be the equivalent of an ordinary week—or at the very least an ordinary day. So that makes thirty days. We've been together for a whole month, then. Is that long enough for you?''

''No, no!'' Jennifer twisted away from him in agitation. ''A month—if it *was* a month—that's nothing. No time at all!''

''Three months, then?''

''No!''

''Six?''

''No!''

''A year?''

She shook her head.

''You play by tough rules. How long *is* long enough, then? Two years? Five? Ten?''

Another brief sideways movement of her head caused two tears to spill from her brimming eyes. She brushed them away hastily, but not before his attentive gaze had detected them. Gently he gathered her in his arms again, turning her toward him so that her bowed head was pillowed on his chest. He said nothing while unchecked tears continued to flow, dampening his shirt. But when she had quieted, he murmured, ''Tell me about it.''

Jennifer didn't respond; couldn't respond. He went on holding her patiently. Gradually she relaxed in the warmth and safety of his arms.

Very quietly, he said, ''This feels nice, doesn't it?''

She nodded affirmatively, sniffled, groped for and found a tissue in her jeans pocket.

"I can see you've had a bad time," Travis went on when she was nestled quietly in his arms again. The unexpected sympathy in his voice was like the soothing coolness of an icy compress on a scorched finger.

"I suppose it was some man," he said. She said nothing, her very lack of denial indicating assent.

"What did he do—make a lot of promises he didn't keep?"

Still she didn't reply. This time he let the silence go on until she felt compelled to answer.

"It—it wasn't like that," she said at last. "Not at all."

He let more time tick slowly by before he asked, "What *was* it like?"

Any pressure, the least hint of demand in his voice would have effectively sealed her lips. But its caressing mildness served to coax her gently onward, until at last the reluctant words began to come. "I...loved someone...for a long time...." Her voice trailed off as resolution failed her.

He waited.

"And then...I saw him again. It was like looking at a stranger. I finally realized that I didn't love him after all." Her words dried up again.

He prompted her gently. "When did all this begin?"

"Oh, years and years ago," Jennifer replied dismally.

"How many years would that be?"

"Seven. Not quite seven." She sniffled again.

"But you were just an infant that long ago."

"No, I wasn't. I was almost eighteen," she said, stiffening a little.

Now it was Travis's turn to be silent. After a while, he said, "Didn't you ever suspect that it might be just a schoolgirl infatuation you felt?"

"Never." She was positive. "I never doubted that it was the real thing. I hated my mother for moving us to Fort Worth, dragging me away."

"And yet you stayed away for a long, long time," he pointed out.

"At the beginning, I hadn't any way of getting back here, short of running away and hitchhiking."

"Couldn't he have sent you money?" he said.

"I never heard from him," she confessed miserably. She forestalled his next question. "I thought my mother intercepted his letters. I thought I might get him in trouble if I showed up on his doorstep. Oh, I don't know now what I thought. That cruel fate was keeping us apart, I guess."

"Was the man married?"

"No, no, nothing like that. It was his job I was worried about—"

"His job?" he prompted again.

But Jennifer had stopped, and she refused to be drawn further. She had come perilously close to naming Claude, perhaps doing him precisely the damage she had feared doing long ago.

Travis seemed to realize that they had strayed into a No Trespassing zone. He took a slightly different tack. "And yet you didn't come back, even when you could have."

"I know," she said drearily. "Somehow I always found a reason. Maybe my subconscious knew it was over, that there was nothing for me here. I only know that consciously I never had any doubts. All those years, that was the central fact of my life. The one thing I knew without question. Perhaps I wasn't completely sure of *his* feelings, but I never once doubted my own." She continued in a faraway voice. "There was a time or two when I thought I was beginning to be in love with someone else, but nothing ever came of it."

He gave her a gentle shake, reminding her where she was. "Because it was never the right someone else, that was why."

"Maybe. Who knows? I just know now that I'll never be able to be sure of my feelings for *anyone*. How can I, after fooling myself like that? In the back of my mind, I'll always be waiting for it to happen again. Just like this time. Because I know it can disappear, all of the—the—" She groped for the right words.

"The magic?" Travis suggested helpfully.

That was close enough. "Yes, the magic," Jennifer agreed.

"But that could never happen between us," he said.

"Yes, it could."

"Not a chance. The effects of magic trout *never* wear off, believe me."

How could he treat it so lightly?—as though it had been a mere girlish crush—this shock that had been like a blow over the heart to her, one from which she felt she might never recover. She moved her shoulders a little crossly. "It's no joking matter."

"I know. But you are being terribly hard on yourself, just because you finally outgrew a youthful infatuation. Now you're all grown up and gorgeous, and no man in his right mind would ever let you slip away from him."

His words did nothing to soothe her ruffled feelings. With a spurt of temper she tensed herself to push him away, to tear herself from his embrace. But the thought brought a coldness to her heart that stopped her, even as she placed a hand against his chest to thrust him back. She paused there, her muscles rigid.

Her sudden movement signaled that he had gone too far. He let her go; he was the one to move away. He retreated to the hearth and stood with his back to the fire, looking down at her.

To his logical mind, it seemed that there *was* no problem. Jennifer was imagining difficulties where none existed. He opened his mouth to explain that to her, soberly and sensibly. But a second thought held him silent. He realized that he had almost made a grave mistake. Her reaction—or overreaction—had come from some deep emotional turmoil. Words of calm reasonableness would never reach her through that kind of a barrier. Not until she was ready to hear them.

Travis glanced around in exasperation. The fire was burning low again. Its flickering light left the far corners of the room in darkness. Heavy shadows moved restlessly around them, turning solid furniture into shapeless phantoms. The glow of the coals lent a reddish otherworldly tinge to the objects it highlighted. Nothing seemed normal and ordinary. For one mad moment he felt that the solution to his dilemma was to stride around the room and snap on every electric light in the place. To let in the harsh light of reason to shrivel these emotional fantasies.

Even as the idea came to him, he rejected it. Shock tactics might only make matters worse. He was keenly aware that their isolated time together was running out. Outside, the storm was dying. Soon the world would crowd in on them, the roads would open. One wrong word and she could be gone, putting thousands of miles between them. Travis clenched his hands in frustration. He knew she was making a profound mistake, but he felt powerless to convince her that he was right and she was wrong.

For lack of other inspiration, he bent down and piled all of the remaining logs on the fire. He arranged them carefully so that bright yellow flames leaped upward to drive back some of the gloom.

He straightened up, dusting off his hands. "Looks like I'd better bring in some more fuel."

On his way to the garage he made it a point to turn on the hall light and the kitchen lights—and left them burning when he returned with an armload of wood. The illumination, though indirect, went a little way toward restoring a feeling of normalcy to the shadowy expanse of the big living room.

He dropped his burden in the wood box. In a light impersonal tone of voice, he said, "The new lodge will have the biggest fireplace on the mountain."

Jennifer looked up at him, surprised and grateful at the change of subject. "You're going ahead with it, then. When did you make the decision?"

"Darned if I know," he confessed. "It just sneaked up on me, I guess."

"Decisions can do that, sometimes," she agreed quickly, then regretted the hasty words, afraid that he might think she was referring to their discussion about Claude. Only he didn't know that it was about Claude, of course. Oh, dear. Her mind scrabbled to find something—anything—that would steer a course safely away from further argument. She glanced around her, at the wide blank windows. "I— I don't hear the wind anymore," she said. The weather was a weak topic, but it would have to do until she could think of something better.

"No, it's almost died away," Travis agreed. "And the clouds are breaking up, too. It's going to be cold, crisp and beautiful out there." After a moment's silence, he added, "Hot tubs were made for nights like this."

"Hot tubs..." Jennifer's voice trailed off a little dubiously.

"We'll look up and count the stars. And chill our champagne in the nearest snowbank."

"Champagne?" she breathed. There was a question in her voice, but a little shiver of anticipation told her that this was a decision her heart had already made.

Chapter Fifteen

I suppose I could wear Darla's terry cloth robe,"
Jennifer said, a little tremulously. "It would be
rather short, but otherwise—" Her voice failed her.

"You could wear mine if you'd rather." Travis's
eyes were dancing. "And *I'll* wear Darla's."

She laughed then and her fears retreated, faded
into the far distance where she could scarcely recognize them. They didn't disappear but stayed
crouched on the edge of the horizon, waiting for tomorrow.

Jennifer knew that she had agreed to more than
just a pleasant interval of soaking in the hot water

and gazing up at the stars. She knew, and she was willing that it should be so. She was as keenly aware as he was that their time together would soon come to an end. Though the night was dark outside, the machinery of the world was marching inexorably toward them. All too soon the roads would be cleared, the telephones connected—and the magic would vanish. No matter what he said, she wouldn't fool herself about that.

Jennifer laughed again, a little feverishly, and put out her hand so he could help her up. In her room, as she traded her clothes for slippers and robe, she felt as though she were standing outside her body, watching someone else gather up her thick dark mass of hair, twisting it and pinning it in place atop her head with steady hands.

This feeling of dislocation persisted until she met Travis in the lower hallway, the champagne bottle cradled in one arm, two stemmed crystal goblets in his hand. His eyes smiled down into hers, and she slipped back into her own skin again, glad to be there, glad to be here—with him.

The path he had shoveled through the hip-high snowdrift was narrow. As they walked in single file, she felt the cold strike her skin with unexpected bite. Most of the lights, positioned as they were at the level of the deck, were buried deep beneath the snow. Only a pair were left to shine feebly through the drifts. The stars blazed out bright and cold in the black velvet sky above them, and once her eyes had adjusted, the white world all around seemed to reflect back their light.

He set the glasses upright on the bench and left them there while he nestled the bottle deep into the snow. She waited until he straightened up and turned back to her, then she loosened her belt and slid the robe from her shoulders. There was no haste or embarrassment in her movements as she bared her body to his gaze. They had already shared an intimacy that went beyond such considerations.

He followed her down the three steps, down into the shock of the waist-deep hot water and into the heat of a passionate embrace. Their two bodies melted together as they kissed, oblivious of the white steam rising and curling around them. After an immeasurable period of time, a minute or an eternity, the bitter coldness of the air made itself felt. Eventually it proved too insistent for even love to ignore. Travis sank down onto the hot tub seat, pulling Jennifer down beside him. Delicious swirling warmth enveloped their shoulders and canceled out the chill. Fingers entwined, they stretched out their legs and slowly, luxuriously tipped their heads back against the headrest, silently looking up into the cold fire of the stars above them.

The moving caress of the water was like a drug, relaxing her body, blurring her thoughts, soothing away the regrets of yesterday and blocking out all fears of tomorrow. Jennifer surrendered to the moment, to the night.

After a long, heavenly time, she roused herself from her languor to turn her head, to gaze at him through heavy-lidded eyes.

He was looking off into the distance, frowning slightly.

"Is anything wrong?" she said.

"I was just thinking," he said, without turning to look at her. "It looks as though I've made a terrible mistake."

For a minute her heart seemed to stop. "You have?" she said, feeling a chill that no hot water could dispel.

"I'm afraid so. Whatever possessed me to leave the champagne over there out of reach? Do you realize what I'll have to go through to get that bottle?"

Jennifer laughed with giddy relief. "Yes, I see your problem. You'll probably break the record for the ten-foot dash."

"And the hop, skip and jump record as well."

She laughed again. "And I thought that a financier was supposed to plan ahead for every contingency."

"That's always been my strong point," Travis agreed solemnly. "Plan Ahead MacKay they call me in the business."

"Then what went wrong this time?"

"I think—" he said judiciously "—I think I was distracted." Suddenly he swooped toward her through the water and gathered her into a bear hug. "And I do believe that I've got my hands on the culprit." He slid one hand down the smooth skin of her side, from the curve of her breast to the swell of her hip. "In fact, I'm working on making a positive identification right now."

She pressed against him. "What a good idea," she murmured. "It would never do to accuse an innocent bystander, would it?"

His hand slid upward again and cupped her breast firmly. "This is the guilty party. I recognize it beyond a doubt. I'd love to give it a hello kiss, but all this infernal hot water is in the way."

"I think I know just how you feel," she said as desire awoke with urgency inside her.

"Do you really?"

"Yes," she breathed. "Yes, I do."

"In that case," he said, and stopped. Then after a long pause he added, "In that case, I'll race you back to the house."

Jennifer tried to pull away. "You'll what?"

"It's the only way we'll get ourselves out of here—on the run and no pausing to think."

"Do we have to go in now?"

"No, we don't have to." His face was very close, his lips caressing her cheek. "But I think it's time, don't you?"

She relaxed against him. "I'm afraid you're right."

"I'll even give you a head start." His hands slipped down to her waist. He turned her away from him so that she faced the steps of the hot tub. She moved easily, buoyed up by the water. "Take a deep breath," he said. "Get set for the next event—the bathrobe wrap, the slipper grab and the snowbank dash! Ready?"

She nodded, and Travis gave a tremendous shove that exploded her out of the water and halfway up the steps. She reached for her robe, flung it around her shoulders and stabbed her feet into her slippers. Laughing, she ran through the narrow pathway in the snow and half fell into the light and warmth of the hall. He was right behind her.

"No fair," she said when she had recovered her breath. "You left your slippers behind."

"But I took time for the important things." He thrust the cold bottle and glasses into her hands and swung her up into his arms. She put her arms around his neck without protest, nestling her head against his shoulder in contentment. One too-hastily-donned slipper dangled from her slender foot, then fell, unnoticed, as he carried her up the stairs.

He dumped her unceremoniously on the big bed then vanished into the bathroom and reappeared almost at once with a huge cinnamon-colored bath towel. They dried each other off, rubbing briskly, with much laughter, sometimes tugging at opposite ends of the towel like playful puppies.

At last, gasping, Jennifer abandoned the game. She lay back on the bed, surrendering wholeheartedly to the keener delights that were yet to come.

"Here, sit up and hold these glasses," he commanded.

It wasn't champagne she had been anticipating. She took the glasses without enthusiasm. "I'm not sure I care for any right now," she said.

"After I abandoned my slippers and risked pneumonia to bring this in from the cold? Of course we're going to have some." He popped the cork and filled the glasses as she held them. "Now—what shall we drink to?"

Travis's eyes met hers, and his gay mood almost faltered. Neither of them wanted to drink to the future. There was nothing for them to toast except this present moment.

"I don't know," she said. She held up the glass, searching for inspiration. "How about—here's to Plan Ahead MacKay—"

"No good. I know something much better to toast." Travis touched the edge of his glass gently against hers. The crystal made a tiny ringing sound. "Here's to the distractions." Very deliberately, he dropped his gaze to Jennifer's naked breasts.

She sipped the champagne, more conscious of his eyes roaming her body than of the taste of the wine. She felt her skin grow rosy under his possessive, provocative scrutiny.

He set down his empty glass, and took her half-full one from her unresisting fingers. "There is something I've been wanting to do," he said. He moved close beside her and reached out gently and deliberately to remove the pins from her hair, pausing as each loosened tress slid down to rest on her bare tanned shoulders. He ran his hand sensuously through the mass of dark silky waves. "Mmm," he said. "I've been imagining this hair spread out on a pillow...those eyes looking up at me...."

He pressed her back onto the bed. She put her arms around him and drew him down with her. Her mouth sought his, hungry and demanding. His lips brushed hers in light butterfly kisses, then touched her eyelids, her throat and breasts before returning to crush her mouth with an urgency of passion that inflamed her own.

His fingertips explored her body with a feathery touch that seemed to leave burning traceries in its wake. That touch was light, so very light, and yet as he persisted it became ever more tantalizing, more arousing.

She clutched at him, at his strong arms, his smoothly muscled back, as deep fires smoldered within her. And the relentless, irresistible touch of his fingers continued, stroking the softness of her skin, her hidden places, bringing them alive until they were quivering with the force of her desire, aching, hungering to feel his forceful strength, his maleness. Longing for them to bear down on her and bear her away.

Her body tried to press itself against his, closer, harder, to lose itself and become one with his. When Travis finally took her, she responded with soaring delight, meeting his strong thrusts with a passion of her own that swelled and built and grew until it claimed her completely in its final explosion, a fusion of the mind and heart and consciousness as well as of the flesh.

Afterward, they lay together in the mutual relaxation of satisfied desire, his arm limp across her body.

Jennifer could feel herself smiling, her whole body warm with happiness as she drifted into sleep.

Chapter Sixteen

The telephone on the bedside table shrilled insistently. Dazzling sunlight poured through the broad window. Travis groped, swearing, for the source of the noise. "Yes," he muttered into the receiver.

"Isn't it marvelous!" Darla's happy voice caroled down the line. "It's *powder*! Honest-to-goodness powder!"

"Darla?" All at once his voice sounded fully awake. Jennifer, still drugged with sleep and squinting against the blinding white light, marveled at the swift transition.

"Wasn't that some storm! Nearly three feet of new snow! And not just any old snow but beautiful, heavenly powder!"

"Is everything all right at the lodge?" Travis was entirely alert and businesslike now, Jennifer saw with a growing feeling of dismay. In fact, he sounded suspiciously like his old self—his before-the-storm self. She watched from her pillow as he hitched himself up until he was half sitting, leaning back against the headboard.

"Everything's great. We had a super time. Just fourteen of us, all snowed in with nothing to do but eat and talk and sit around the fire. Did you two make out all right without any groceries? I bet you were reduced to eating the olives for the martinis—"

"We managed," her brother interjected briefly, catching Jennifer's eye with a conspiratorial smile for the memory of candlelit dining and magic trout. She tried to smile back, but in the harsh light of morning those tempestuous hours seemed to be fading, slipping from her grasp.

"Don't worry another minute where your next meal is coming from," Darla went on. "The snowplows won't have made it up to our road yet, but Claude is making arrangements to get you out of there the very first thing this morning." Exuberantly she sang, "They'll be down to getcha in a snowmobile, honey," then broke off to add, almost crossly, "half the instructors in the ski school just walked in. Everybody's crazy to get out there on that fresh powder. And Claude's already given orders to start grooming the slopes. I'd better get out there before they track it all up."

"Let me talk to Claude before you go," Travis said quickly.

Jennifer slipped out of bed. She didn't want to listen to any more of this.

She showered quickly, half wishing he would join her, half dreading that he might. His conversation with Claude kept him long enough for her to be dressed in her jeans and Darla's off-the-shoulder sweater by the time he came to her door.

A shadow of disappointment crossed his face. Jennifer went on combing her hair, pretending to concentrate on her image in the mirror. She felt as though she were being torn in two. With all her heart she wanted him to take her in his arms, to turn the clock back to yesterday, to make tomorrow go away. But she could plainly see the doors swinging slowly closed on all of that. The bright and wonderful time was over.

The outside world had come crowding in on them, starting with the first ring of the telephone. Next there would be the snowmobiles and the lodge and Claude. And then Travis would be gone—on a plane to Kansas City or somewhere—and in the end she would be left alone. Alone to cope with her knowledge of the fickleness of her own heart.

She put down her hairbrush. "What did Claude have to say?" she asked, knowing it could be nothing that she wanted to hear.

Travis smiled wryly. "Knowing that we must be desperate to get away from here, he has cobbled together an elaborate plan to ferry us out. Some of the men are loading a couple of snowmobiles on a four-wheel-drive truck. They'll drive up as far as they can go, depending on how far the snowplows have cleared the highway. With any luck, they might get as far as the beginning of our private road. Then they'll offload the snowmobiles, drive the rest of the way up here, pick us up and take us down to the truck. After all that, there didn't seem to be any way to break it to him that we were happy where we were."

Jennifer looked down at her hands. "Well," she said, a little unsteadily, "at least there'll be something besides fish for breakfast."

He crossed the room to her, passing through a patch of sunshine that splashed him with a brightness that vanished with the next step. She rose to meet him, to shelter in the arms that reached out for her, to rest her head against his shoulder one more time. This was love, she was sure of it. As sure as ever she had been that she loved Claude—and look what had come of that. She had to open her hands and let it go. She couldn't clutch it to her, to awaken every morning knowing that this might be the day that love would die. Perhaps someday she would be reckless enough to take the chance. But not this time. This was too precious to take risks with.

"I won't listen to a word against fish," Travis said grandly. "We should put up a monument to trout. On the other hand, I don't have any prejudice against bacon and eggs either, I must admit."

"And buttered toast and fresh orange juice," she said, trying for a light tone of voice to match his own.

"Not to mention hot muffins. And jam. And a big stack of hotcakes."

"That reminds me of something. What would you say to a frozen waffle, toasted of course? Only there's nothing to put on it, is there? Unless you'd like a little marmalade to perk it up? We could manage that."

His arms tightened around her. "Sometimes, I think it's possible to worry too much about what we're going to eat next. There are other things in the world besides cheese omelets and jelly doughnuts. For instance—" He slid his hand down to the hollow of her waist, pressing her body against his. He bent his head, but Jennifer turned her face away from his seeking lips.

"I'd better pack," she said distractedly. "My overnight bag's not very big. I suppose they can take it on a snowmobile, can't they?"

"I'm sure they'll manage. But there's no hurry," he replied as she pushed away from him. "They probably haven't even left the lodge yet."

She picked up her small suitcase and laid it on the bed as she unfastened the clasps. She raised the lid. He shut it again with a firm hand.

"What's the matter?" Travis asked.

"Nothing's the matter." If those clear gray eyes were going to keep looking at her so compellingly, she would never be able to manage her thoughts or her emotions, to keep them clear and intelligible. If only the telephone would ring again and summon him away. But nothing like that happened. She cast about for another way to get the two of them out of the bedroom.

"Coffee," she said suddenly. "I'm dying for some coffee. And I'm sure you are, too. I'll go down and make some while you dress. You wouldn't want to be still in your bathrobe when they get here." She moved quickly to the door and only looked back from the hallway—to see him still standing beside the bed, watching her go.

Jennifer went down the stairs more slowly, listening for footsteps behind her. Perversely, she felt disappointed to hear him cross to his own room, perhaps to take her advice and get ready for the up-coming trip.

She fixed her coffee—a spoonful of dark powder in the cup, a minute and a half in the microwave—and marveled that he had let her get away with that bold-faced statement about making coffee while he dressed. She drank it slowly, standing in front of the living-room window, watching the last of the clouds being wiped away from the blue face of the sky. The sunlit world glistened and flashed diamond-bright. An untouched blanket of snow reflected the rays of the sun in eye-dazzling brilliance.

The beauty of the scene was lost on her. All her attention was focused behind her as she listened, every nerve ending alert, for the sound of his approach.

Everything was so different in the strong light of day. It seemed to drain some of the color from the room and to point up the film of dust that was beginning to gather on polished surfaces. The gaiety and excitement had fled with the coming of dawn. The first ring of the telephone had signaled a return to the drabness of daily life. The warm firelight that had turned the hearth into a little island of enchantment was now nothing but gray ashes in the grate.

She was telling herself all of these things—and then he stepped into the room. The air between them crackled with all the old tensions, and her heart beat faster.

He came to stand just behind her. She knew it without turning her head. She didn't need eyes to see him; her skin knew where he was.

Jennifer braced herself to marshal her arguments anew, to stand up to his demands. She decided on exactly the light, unemotional tone of voice to use. She waited. But he didn't speak, and at last she was forced to break the unnatural silence herself.

"When we get back to the lodge," she said, "Darla can tell us exactly where she left her Porsche, and I'll ask Claude to have someone take me down to it so I can get my things out of the trunk."

"If that's what you want," he said in a cool tone that struck icily at her heart.

Travis had been thinking long and hard about their situation during the time he had been alone upstairs. It seemed that the more he argued with her, the more stubborn she became. He had sold a lot of ideas in his career; surely he ought to be able to persuade one desirable young woman to believe what her heart was already telling her! Perhaps he was pushing her too hard. It could be that the wisest thing to do now was to do nothing at all—to take the pressure off. For lack of any other way to reach her, that was what he had determined to try.

"I must go upstairs and pack." She spoke as coolly as he had.

When she had gone, he made a cup of coffee and drank it moodily, standing in front of the big windows as she had done. If only their time together weren't so limited. Once she was free of this cage of snow, only a miracle would make her stay, he was thinking when he finally heard the piercing sound of snowmobiles. They were still faraway, but coming closer at top speed.

Fresh cold air swept into the house with the two young men from the lodge, along with laughter and high spirits and brisk efficiency. Claude had even provided a parka for Jennifer, a man's parka, big enough to wear over her own jacket. It covered her to midthigh.

They rode through a landscape of motionless crystal beauty to where the truck waited on the plowed highway. The air was like wine, icy and delicious. Jennifer felt it was a pity to crowd into the cab of the truck for the ride to the lodge, but she said nothing. There was no chance for private conversation between them on the way, of course. And Claude was there to greet them when the truck pulled into the parking lot.

He looked much more relaxed than when she had seen him before—and much happier. So Travis must have given him the go-ahead on the lodge expansion during their telephone conversation earlier this morning.

"Such a day!" Claude greeted them expansively. "One in a thousand!"

Through snow piled waist-high on either side of them, they picked their way along the cleared path to the lodge door. Behind them, a solitary snowplow in the parking lot was working at the job of clearing the huge expanse of blacktop, laboriously piling snow in mountainous heaps around the perimeter.

"Three feet of new snow!" Claude put his arm around Jennifer's shoulders as he steered them down the hall toward the stairs to the dining room. She didn't know whether it was an unconscious gesture, born of his unusual exuberance of spirit, or whether it was a deliberate one, made to reassert a prior claim to her affections.

Chapter Seventeen

"Where's Darla?" asked Jennifer, as they sat down to the elaborate breakfast Claude had arranged for them.

Claude gestured toward the windows, to where the mountain loomed, dazzling in its fresh mantle of white. "Need you ask?" he replied.

Travis looked up from his plate. "Knowing her, I expect she has gone where no skis have gone before. She's a fiend for untracked snow."

"Exactly," said Claude. He was sitting across the table from Jennifer, toying with a cup of coffee. She was aware of his eyes on her, but also aware that the businessman in him was being suppressed only with great effort. He managed the polite small talk well enough, but an occasional lapse of attention on his part made it plain that he was itching to get down to the plans for the expansion of Highlands.

She was still amazed that she could look at this man with such a dispassionate eye. Where had all that wild emotion disappeared to? If seven years could steal that away, what was there left to depend upon? She could even criticize him now, admitting all the doubts she had refused to permit herself before. Why had he let her go? Why had he never written? How could she have been such a fool? Where love was concerned, she didn't have sense enough to be allowed out on her own. In the midst of all this internal dialogue, she ate the good food that was placed in front of her. But she tasted none of it.

She looked covertly to her right, stealing a glance at Travis. He was eating with relish while keeping up his end of the conversation with Claude. It was a more vigorous, lively conversation, now that the subject had somehow slid around to the exact site of the restaurant that was to be located at the gondola terminus.

Jennifer barely heard the talk, was glad to be left out of it. She was thinking that she didn't even have a photograph of Travis to take away with her. Why had she ever let herself be separated from her cameras? It seemed that she couldn't look back on one single sensible action on her own part from the moment she'd arrived at this place. She must leave, must get away from here before her last shred of self-confidence disappeared.

She waited for a lull in their talk to ask, "Do you know just where Darla's Porsche is now, Claude?"

Travis gave her a quick glance. She noticed but refused to acknowledge it.

"I've no idea," said Claude. "In a ditch off the main highway somewhere, I understand. And well hidden under the snow, no doubt. As yours is, *chérie*, here in our parking lot."

All of the vehicles that had been trapped here during the storm were now mere featureless mounds of snow. The Porsche, sunk in its anonymous ditch, might be even more deeply buried by the snow that the plows had removed from the road. Without Darla's help, there would be no chance of finding it before a thaw. All at once Jennifer felt an overwhelming need to have her own possessions about her. A change of clothes, the freedom to come and go as she pleased, her very livelihood—they were all out of her reach.

"I *must* talk to Darla," she said. "I must have my things."

Claude's smile was affectionate, his shrug very French.

"You can page her on the loudspeakers," Jennifer persisted. "Tell her it's important, that she must come in."

"Yes, of course," Claude said, "We could do that." He looked to Travis for agreement.

Travis nodded for him to go ahead. But the rueful look that passed between the two men spoke louder than any words. Darla could be summoned, but no one could guarantee that she would come.

The message went out over the speakers posted along the ski runs, but in half an hour, then an hour, there was no response.

Jennifer paced the floor of Claude's office as the two men watched her.

"It's lunchtime," Claude pointed out helpfully. "Perhaps she will come in to eat."

Jennifer turned to Travis. He had leaned back in the big shabby leather chair and stretched his long legs into the center of the room, but the sharpness of his eyes belied his relaxed posture.

"We've passed the word," he said. "Anyone who sees her will tell her that she's wanted at the lodge."

"She must know that much by now. It's being broadcast all over the mountain," Jennifer said sharply.

"It's warming up very rapidly," Claude put in. "There's a lot of heat in that sun. And they say a Chinook is on the way."

The Chinook. Jennifer remembered it well. The unseasonal warm wind of winter. The Snoweater, the Indians called it. "Do you propose that we just sit here until the snow melts enough to spoil the skiing, in the hope that that will bring her in?"

"What else can we do, short of going up and looking for her ourselves?" Claude inquired.

"That's a very good suggestion," Jennifer commented. "Have either of you considered that she might be hurt?"

Claude and Travis exchanged glances again. Clearly, they both found it infinitely more probable that Darla was simply enjoying herself to the exclusion of all else and would continue on her heedless way until she got hungry or tired or bored enough to come in on her own.

"I've had the lift boys questioning everyone who goes up," Travis told them. "No one remembers seeing her for the last hour or so."

"She could be down on one of the cross trails," said Jennifer. "She may need help."

Her growing alarm finally communicated itself to them. Travis got to his feet with an air of decision. He nodded to Claude. "Yes, I think we've waited long enough. There's a possibility that Jennifer may be right. We'd better have a full-scale search."

"I'll send out the ski patrol," Claude offered. "And everyone else who is available."

Travis stared out the window as though expecting to see his young sister come sailing down the slope. He frowned at the bland, smiling face of the mountain. "I'll get some skis and go along."

"And I'll go with you," said Jennifer.

Travis had made the snowmobile trip in his gleaming black ski suit, but Jennifer had to borrow suitable clothes for their mission from one of the taller ski instructors. The other girl's white bib overall style ski pants fitted her sleekly, but the white and red jacket was too narrow across the shoulders and restricted her arm movements. Jennifer hurriedly shrugged out of it and grabbed up the roomy man's parka that Claude had sent to the house for her.

Travis was faintly uneasy about Darla's failure to put in an appearance but still far from convinced that anything except his sister's own blithe heedlessness was to blame. On such a perfect day for skiing, it was easy to picture her up there hiding, like a naughty child when the grown-ups call her in from play.

The lift chairs swayed gently as they traveled up the slope of the intermediate run called Haywire. Travis turned to look at Jennifer in the seat beside him, her eyes closed, her face turned up to the warm kiss of the sun. Her long lashes brushed the perfect curve of her cheek. Travis willed her to open her eyes and speak to him, to bridge the gap that had opened between them with the coming of morning. He was only too aware that her urgency to recover her suitcases could easily be translated into an equal urgency to be gone from Highlands. But they could hardly talk of those things now. His mind was chaotic but his eyes were alert, constantly checking the terrain below them for any sign of Darla.

Jennifer stirred in the seat beside him. He turned back to her to see the sapphire eyes also scanning the slope in troubled concentration.

"What color is she wearing?" she asked him.

"Claude said she's wearing bright red."

"That should make her easier to spot," she said, then fell silent, as though acknowledging the tension created by the unresolved problems between them.

They skied quickly away from the lift but stopped uncertainly at the top of the run. The sun of early afternoon reflected blindingly off the glistening snow. The temperature was unnaturally high. Travis unzipped his parka and absently stuffed his gloves and cap into his pockets as he pondered where to begin the search. Highlands took in a lot of territory, dozens of bowls and meadows, connecting trails and ridges.

"This lift and Widowmaker are the only two that have been operating," he said, half to himself, half to Jennifer who was waiting beside him. "But that doesn't mean that she has to be on either of these runs. Someone would have seen her by now if she were here. She must have ridden to the top here and then crossed over to one of the others. Claude has organized the ski patrol and the other searchers and sent them out to cover specific sectors. So, I guess that leaves the two of us on our own." He glanced around, seeking some clue, some indication of the path to take. "Now, where would you go if you were Darla?"

Jennifer looked down the long white slope, crossed and crisscrossed with the tracks of earlier skiers. A vagrant thought stirred in her memory.

"I think we should take a look at Three Mile Canyon," she said slowly.

"Why do you say that?"

"Darla spoke of it the other night."

He frowned. "But that's avalanche country. She wouldn't go there, not when the skiing is so excellent right here."

Jennifer gestured at the no longer pristine whiteness below them. "You said yourself that she's a fiend for untracked snow. Perhaps this just whetted her appetite for an entire snowfield she could have all to herself.''

"There are times when she wouldn't win any prizes for common sense," he said, "but she knows better than to go into a place like that by herself."

"All the same," said Jennifer, "she spoke of the avalanche patrol making a run to clear the danger spots after every storm. Perhaps she doesn't realize that they'll have all they can do to clear the cross-country ski trails today. I think I'll go over there and make sure no one has passed that way."

She pushed off toward the nearest connecting trail. After a moment's hesitation he followed. "Did anyone ever tell you that you can be a damnably stubborn person?" he said.

She turned to look at him. "Yes," she said. "My mother told me that a few years back." It had been seven years ago, to be exact, but she kept that information to herself.

They had a long trek to the canyon, most of it crosswise to the slope of the mountain rather than downhill. Tracks in the snow ahead of them showed that several skiers had also passed this way. But that proved nothing, for other, safer meadows branched off in this direction, too. The final approach to Three Mile Canyon was along a high bleak ridge where the wind had apparently blown the snow away almost as fast as it had come down. The sun had melted off what little had been left. Pockets of snow still lingered in some of the depressions in the rock. In one such pocket they found a straight groove that was undoubtably the mark of a ski. Straight ahead of them a sign said NO SKIING IN THIS AREA. Jennifer waited for him to insist that Darla would never have ignored such a warning, but by now he was grimly silent.

At last they came to the rim of the canyon and looked down at a gleaming, sugar-frosted slope beneath them. It was steep, enticing and coldly dangerous. There were no tracks to be seen. An occasional huge boulder was the only thing that marred the unblemished perfection of the snow. They circled around the rim, and in a few minutes, Jennifer pointed and cried out with relief.

"Look! It's safe! The avalanche has come down. It's all right now!"

A wide section of snow was no longer perfect but spilled down in a rumpled mass from just under the canyon rim. As they came abreast of the ragged swath, they could see that just beyond it a set of ski tracks dipped into the canyon, swooping in great, graceful curves. It needed no effort of imagination to conclude that Darla had followed the rim just as they were doing, and once she had seen that the avalanche had passed, she had tipped over the edge and carved her bliss into that hillside of perfect powder.

Chapter Eighteen

Jennifer flashed Travis a smile of heartfelt relief. "She may be hurt, but at least she wasn't caught in an avalanche. We'll be able to find her." She stepped forward onto the fresh snow, dug in her poles and pushed off, following Darla's tracks down into the canyon. The fine powder foamed about her knees. It was like skiing on a cloud—and almost as effortless.

Suddenly Travis flashed past her. The snow rose up in a long plume behind him as he skied ahead of her and cut her off, forcing her to a stop.

"What's the matter?" she gasped, shaken. "Why did you do that?"

"You have to go back," he said. "This entire sector is a potential avalanche slope."

She looked around her, uncomprehending. The snowfield around them seemed completely peaceful, a hidden world of the finest fresh powder snow a skier could dream of. An invitation that was hard to resist. And ahead of them, to beckon them onward, were the marks of Darla's untroubled passage.

Travis's frown deepened. She could see that he was now more worried than before. "That slope in back of us obviously avalanched hours ago," he said. "But another spot could let loose anywhere along here. The least disturbance could set it off. A loud noise, the cutting edge of a ski, a skier's weight—anything. No patrolman has been around to dynamite the danger spots today. The whole place is poised and ready to let go."

It was hard to believe, but the urgency in his voice convinced her. Darla must have come along here earlier by the same path they had traveled. She would have seen the spot where the avalanche had happened—and then she too must have jumped to the conclusion that the canyon had been swept and was safe.

"What shall we do?" Jennifer asked in a small voice.

"Someone has to go for help," he said grimly. "Back to the lift shack at the top of Haywire. Call Claude from there and tell him what's happened."

Jennifer looked at him with eyes that were wide with dismay. It would take time to retrace their path all the way back to the lift shack. It was already midafternoon, and the days were short this time of year. Soon the sun would dip below the canyon's rim, and the cold blue shadows would well up to engulf everything—and everyone—inside it. The November night would come early to Three Mile Canyon. All of her instincts were to go forward. If Darla needed help, she needed it now, not hours away.

She read in his eyes what he meant to do, and insubordination flared up in her. "You're not going to go on alone! I may not know much about avalanche territory, but I do know that the very worst thing you can do is tackle it by yourself."

His mouth set in a stubborn line. "It will take time to spread the word and to get a proper search team in here. Maybe hours. And that might be too long. I *have* to go on. I can't leave when I know she needs help."

"Then I'm going with you," Jennifer said quietly.

"Don't make it worse than it already is, Jennifer. I can't take you into this kind of danger."

"You aren't taking me. I'm taking myself." She wouldn't listen to any further argument. How could she turn back to safety, knowing that Travis would be risking his life? Somewhere deep inside she had the irrational conviction, more a feeling than a coherent thought, that he couldn't disappear under the snow as long as she was there to watch over him. The idea of danger to herself hardly occurred to her. She had faith in his strength and competence; he would keep her safe. And her presence would protect him. He wouldn't be as reckless with her life as he might be with his own.

"Go back," he said. "Please."

Jennifer shook her head. "I can't leave her, either." To show her determination, she moved sideways, as though to proceed around him.

He stopped her with a hand on her arm.

"Stubborn," Travis said, without a smile. But there was resignation in his voice. "Well, then, let's get properly organized first." He took his knit hat out of his pocket and put it on. "Put on your hat and gloves," he told her, following his own instructions as he spoke. "Pull up your parka hood and zip up all your zippers. Unbuckle your safety straps and take your hands out of your pole loops. If the snow should let go under you, it will grab you and twist you, and you don't want to give it the least bit of extra leverage to work with. The hat and gloves and hood will help to conserve warmth."

When they were both ready, he pointed to the slope in front of them. "Up ahead, there will be more steep slopes like this one. We have here a fresh, heavy snowfall and a sudden rise in temperature—that's a classic avalanche configuration. If ever you feel the snow letting go under your skis, go as fast as you can—ski like hell—for the far edge. Try to ski out of it. If it should pull you down, then drop your poles and start to swim with the flow. If—" he took a deep breath "—if you can't stay on top, try as hard as you can to get a hand in front of your face. That will make an airspace so you can breathe."

She listened carefully, but with the vague feeling that although it was all very interesting, it couldn't happen to her—the same feeling she always had when airline stewardesses demonstrated how to use life jackets in case of a plane crash. When he'd finished, she could see that he was about to tell her to stay behind once more, so she faced forward resolutely.

"What do we do now?" she asked.

A hundred yards ahead of them, the steep slope they were on began to gradually level off. Travis pointed to one side, where a gray boulder thrust upward through the snow.

"That should be a secure position," he said. "I'll go first. You wait right here, and don't come any farther until I'm all the way over. The weight of the two of us could be just enough to make it run."

She waited, poised, every nerve alert, as he launched himself across the intervening space. When he reached the safety of the trees and turned to wave her on, she found that she had been holding her breath. She followed, skiing as carefully, as skillfully as she could.

When she was just a few yards short of her goal, the snow suddenly humped up in front of her skis. All at once she was traveling downhill and sideways at alarming speed.

Travis kicked forward onto the flowing mass. His hand closed on her arm in a viselike grip, and he swung her inward toward the rock. Their bodies pressed together as they were brought up short against the boulder. For a long moment they were knee-deep in boiling snow. An undertow clutched at them, fought to drag them down. The air shuddered, cracked like a giant whip about their ears. Then the snow sagged back like a spent wave.

Reverberations traveled along the canyon like a muted roll of thunder. They waited without moving until the silence returned.

"Did I do something wrong?" Jennifer half whispered, shaken by the suddenness with which the snow beneath her feet could shift from an inert substance to a savage and irresistible force.

"No, you did fine," he reassured her. "It was just ready to go, and it went. It should have run with the first skier across, but it just hung fire and waited for the second. Are you all right?"

"Yes, as soon as I get my breath back. It took me by surprise. And where did that tremendous noise come from?"

"That was just displaced air. The avalanche leaves a vacuum behind it and air crashes in to fill up the space." He looked down into her upturned face. "Now do you see that you must go back?"

Now that danger had stepped out of the shadows and onto center stage to exhibit the full power of its menace—that was what he was saying. But to Jennifer that was all the more reason she couldn't leave him to dare it alone. It was a job for two people—or twenty. For a single skier it could be suicide. She forced herself to stand erect and made sure that her voice was steady before she said, "Darla may be just around the next bend. We can't stop now."

At times the canyon broadened out into a basin, a meadow, and there were even some flatter spots where they were forced to walk. But for the most part, they encountered steep, ominous pitches that had to be covered in breath-holding one-at-a-time fashion. Whenever Travis was in the middle of one of these slopes, completely vulnerable to the vagaries of the snow, Jennifer would keep her eyes on him unblinkingly, ready to mark his path if the worst should happen and the snow take him down, ready to go to his rescue. And then she would follow, knowing that he was similarly watching over her.

And always, beckoning them onward, were those wide, curving tracks in the snow that marked Darla's carefree passage.

Darla's tracks ran happily ahead of them across the meadows and down the steep pitches, until Jennifer and Travis looked down at an incline steeper than any of the others had been. Directly in front of them the smooth snow fractured into the wrack and tumble of a wide-scale avalanche. Darla's tracks went right up to the edge—and disappeared.

Jennifer's knees grew weak.

"Come on." Travis didn't hesitate. "It's safe enough now, it won't run twice. She may have come out the other side."

The declining sun was well below the rim of the canyon. The brilliant blue sky had darkened and long fingers of shadow closed around them now, chilling the air, chilling her heart.

"Here," called Travis. "Her tracks are here!"

Ski tracks showed clearly in the undisturbed snow on the other side. But they were mingled with other marks—scuffs and indentations in the snow. Their meaning was inescapable.

"Darla's hurt," Jennifer whispered.

Chapter Nineteen

Jennifer and Travis moved slowly forward in the gathering dusk, trying to make sense of the marks in the snow. The shapeless indentations gradually resolved themselves into a readable pattern. The marks of two poles planted deeply on either side of a single ski and—more ominously—the scuffed trail of a dragging foot.

"She must have injured her left leg," Travis said.

"I'm afraid you're right," said Jennifer. "But it doesn't look like she's hurt badly. The leg's not broken, or she would still be here."

They pressed on quickly through a boulder-strewn basin. Their search ended at last just beyond a shoulder-high rock poised on the edge of the next steep downward pitch. In spite of her own reassuring words, Jennifer felt her heart sink at the sight of a darker heap huddled unmoving in the snow.

"Darla!" Travis sped ahead, breaking his own rule against raising their voices. The dark shape moved, and a pale face turned in their direction. He stooped to put his arms around her, lifted her up. "Are you hurt, Big Eyes? How bad is it?"

"Oh, Trav, I knew you'd come for me! My knee hurts. I twisted it or something." In the poor light, her red ski pants looked almost black, but her red and white knit turtleneck shirt stood out more plainly. There was a pathetically small pile of snow beside her where she had evidently tried to dig herself a snow cave with her one remaining ski.

"You're shivering," said Travis. "You're half-frozen! What happened to your parka?"

Jennifer unzipped the oversize jacket she was wearing and put it around the younger girl's shoulders. Travis wrapped it around her tightly, his encircling arms holding it in place. Jennifer pulled up the hood to cover Darla's hair, feeling the cold strike through her to her own upper body. The knit top she had borrowed had long sleeves, but just like Darla's, it was too lightweight for such low temperatures.

"The snow took my jacket," Darla said through chattering teeth. "It was so hot skiing, there wasn't a breath of air anywhere. So, I took it off and tied it around my waist. Then that snow slid out from under me, and it knocked me down and rolled me over. When I crawled out, my jacket was just gone. And so was one ski. But I couldn't have used it anyway; I can't put my weight on this darn knee." A fit of shivering overtook her, and her voice rose to a wail. "I knew you were coming, Trav—but it took you so *long*! It's getting dark, and I was all alone. I was *scared*!"

"You're not alone any more," he said, his voice grim. Darla leaned against him and was silent. Their mere presence seemed to have put her fears to rest— now it was up to someone else to take care of her. The responsibility of her safety had clearly passed to them.

Travis looked from Darla to Jennifer. He put out an arm and drew her closer, sheltering her against him. Darla shuddered, burrowed against his chest. Jennifer was unable to hold back a sudden fit of shivering that seemed to come from deep inside her as the unrelenting cold penetrated her flesh through the thin sweater.

"This won't do," he said harshly. "I've got to keep you warm. Both of you. Jennifer, put your jacket back on."

Both Jennifer and Darla made an involuntary movement of protest, but he insisted. "Do it. Put your arms in the sleeves." He turned Darla away from him. "Now you slide your arms inside, around Jennifer. Hold her as tight as you can, and I'll see if I can fasten the zipper. This thing looks almost big enough for the two of you."

Darla's ungloved hands felt like cold iron where they touched Jennifer's back. Travis grasped the front edges of the parka, striving to make the two edges of the zipper meet. Jennifer tried to help him, but without success. He had to abandon the attempt.

"Almost big enough, but not quite," he said. He unzipped his own parka and hung it around Darla's shoulders. "How does that feel?"

"Better. Lots better." Darla shivered lightly and continually in Jennifer's embrace, but her voice was stronger than before. "Jennifer feels so *warm*!"

"You're going to be fine," he said. "As long as you can shiver, you aren't into hypothermia. Two can be twice as warm as one, sharing body heat. Now I'm going to unfasten our ski bindings so the two of you can step over to one side while I take a whack at this snow cave that Darla started."

"The snow is too fluffy," said Darla. "I couldn't do a thing with it. And my hands got too cold, so I couldn't hold onto the ski."

They stepped aside awkwardly. He attacked the loose powdery snow, using one of Jennifer's skis as a scoop.

"This is like shoveling feathers in the dark," he said after a few minutes. "It won't be much of a cave, but it'll do part of the job, help you conserve heat." His cheery, reassuring tone of voice alarmed Jennifer more than his words.

She said, "You're not going on alone."

"It's safe enough from here on," he said, in that same unconcerned voice that frightened her so. "The exit from the canyon is probably just around the next curve. And then I'll be skiing through the trees in the moonlight."

Jennifer was silent. She was certain that he knew no more about the terrain ahead than she did.

The edge of a round moon appeared over the canyon rim, lifting the curtain of darkness that hung between them. Travis straightened to his full height and thrust the ski upright in the snow beside the shallow bowl he had managed to scoop out.

"There you are, ladies. A cozy bed in case you nod off in the thirty or forty minutes it should take me to get back with the ski patrol."

The moonlight strengthened, reflecting off the white surface of the snow. Now she could see his face, see the rigid set of his jaw that belied his easy words of comfort.

He put his arms around the two of them. To Jennifer's apprehensive heart, there seemed to be a note of farewell in his embrace.

"You're not going on alone," she repeated fiercely.

"We can't leave her here," he replied, keeping his voice pitched low, as if its very quietness would somehow prevent Darla from guessing the truth.

"One bulging overhang is all it takes—you said it yourself. And if you're alone—"

His eyes met hers with such a savage warning that her impassioned words were cut off.

More calmly, she said, "I'm coming with you."

"You're needed here. You have to keep Darla warm."

They stood close together with Darla between them, like two adults quarreling in unnaturally quiet voices over the head of a drowsy child. Jennifer wanted to retort that it was also important to keep *him* alive. But she knew she mustn't say it—mustn't alarm his little sister—mustn't spoil all his efforts to protect Darla from the knowledge of the danger she had drawn them all into.

Very softly, Jennifer said, "It looks like Three Mile Canyon was one more shiny red toy, doesn't it?"

He overrode her words. "The sooner I leave, the sooner I'll be back." He bent his head protectively toward Darla. "How're you doing, Big Eyes? Feeling any warmer?"

"I think so," she said. "But my knee is hurting pretty bad."

Jennifer realized perfectly well that it would take a sterner heart than her own to leave Darla behind to wait all alone. "Take your jacket," she said to Travis.

"I'll be all right without it. Skiing will keep me plenty warm."

He wouldn't be all right without it if he had to fight his way out of an avalanche, Jennifer knew. He was taking enough of a chance, going on by himself. This added another—unacceptable—risk.

"You wear the jacket," she said with iron determination, "or I go with you."

Darla clutched her more tightly. "Don't leave me."

Jennifer pretended to ignore her, pretending to ignore the anger that blazed in his eyes. "Since it's going to be so simple," she went on implacably, "we'll just wrap Darla up in both of the parkas and snuggle her down here in the snow. And we'll both keep nice and warm skiing for the few minutes it will take to get around the bend and up to the nearest patrol shack. I'll leave Darla my hat and gloves."

"Don't do this," he said, warningly.

"I mean it." Her voice was as unyielding as his. Maybe he felt it was right that he should take on the lion's share of the danger, but he wasn't going to stack the deck completely against his own chances of survival. Not as long as she had anything to say about it.

He stared at her, measuring the strength of her determination.

Jennifer saw his capitulation, read it in the lip-tightening fury that hardened his face before he turned abruptly away from her.

He touched Darla's shoulder in silent apology then took back his parka. He rammed his arms into the sleeves, stamped his boots back into the ski bindings and reached for the ski poles he had thrust upright in the deep snow. Then he left them, pushing off toward the steep slope of the canyon floor.

Jennifer wrapped Darla in the oversize parka as they watched him go, a tall black figure in the moonlight, driving himself relentlessly across the stark white landscape.

Jennifer forced her eyes unnaturally wide, afraid even to blink as she tracked his moonlit progress. An unsuspected fold in the terrain suddenly blocked him from sight. He reappeared in a second, farther down the slope. But in that second, Jennifer felt as though her heart had stopped. It thudded wildly in her chest before it returned to its former steadiness. For that one second she had believed he was gone. From the intensity of the pain that shot through her, she knew how hard it was going to be when the time of parting came.

Quickly he was out of sight, gone from them. Perhaps the parting time had already come, no matter how this adventure turned out. From the look on his face when he turned away, she knew that though he might come back, it would not be to her. Not to someone who had come between him and his sense of obligation to his little sister.

Darla stirred. "Jennifer, I—"

"Hush!" Jennifer cut her off. "Listen!" The stillness of the night settled around them. The silence was so complete that it seemed as though the beat of her anguished heart should be audible across the broad expanse of snow. She had remembered the crack of thunder that came as the aftermath of the earlier avalanche. If they heard nothing, then he should be safe. He might be hating her, but he would be alive.

"I don't hear anything," Darla whispered.

"That means he's all right," said Jennifer. "As long as it stays quiet, he's all right."

They waited without moving while long minutes dragged on, until it felt as though hours must have passed. But the full moon, now riding well clear of the canyon rim, seemed not to have risen the smallest distance farther in the night sky, so Jennifer knew the elapsed time was only a mere handful of minutes. It might be a very long night.

Until he returned with help, it was up to her to do whatever she could for this little five-foot-tall stumbling block to her own happiness. Darla was becoming almost a deadweight in her arms. As the shivering body pressed more and more heavily against her own, she knew that they must not remain standing like this much longer.

She maneuvered them into the scooped-out hollow Travis had made. It was difficult to get Darla positioned with the parka around her and her leg reasonably comfortable, and still enable Jennifer to sit close enough to have some protection from the all-invasive cold. They twisted and experimented until they achieved a passable arrangement that left them facing one another with Jennifer's arms around Darla's waist inside the parka and Darla's arms in the too-long sleeves shielding Jennifer's exposed back.

Jennifer was silent as they worked at this, or as nearly silent as possible. She did not once voice her own fears or her opinion of Darla's actions, but her disapproval apparently came through all too plainly.

When they were settled, Darla spoke with a timidity Jennifer had never heard from her before. "How long do you think Trav will be?" she inquired.

Jennifer bit back the sharp retort that rose to her lips. There was no denying it, there was something about Darla's childishness that made everyone want to protect her, and Jennifer found that she was no exception. If she could feel this way herself in these circumstances, she thought drearily, she shouldn't blame Travis for his attitude, or Darla for being the way she was. If every pill so far has been sugar-coated, it takes a hard-hearted person to be the first one to administer bitter medicine.

"He's been gone a long time," Darla added, half-fearfully, half-hopefully. "Maybe they're on their way back to get us by now."

Jennifer would have liked to believe that, too, if only she could have convinced herself that it was so. But common sense told her it was impossible. She shied away from telling Darla so in blunt terms, but perhaps it was time to at least start treating her as an adult.

"You know the canyon better than I do," she said, trying to keep any flavor of blame out of her voice. "How much time would it take *you* to reach the nearest lift shack from here?"

"I'll have to think about that," Darla said obediently. "Let's see, I guess we're at least halfway down, two-thirds, maybe. But the last part is pretty flat. Even Trav won't make much speed along there. And the exit trail is hard to spot—it'll be even harder in the dark. Trav will find it," she said loyally.

"And then how long to reach the nearest lift shack?" Jennifer prompted her.

"It's not very far. He could be there in maybe half an hour from the time he left us. Or forty-five minutes, anyway. With any luck."

And if luck was against them he might never reach it, but of course it was unthinkable to mention that. "Then he'll use the lift shack telephone to call for help...." Jennifer prompted her again.

"Yes, and then they'll have to get the rescue team together and bring out the sleds...and drag them all the way up here." Discouragement crept into Darla's voice. Then she brightened. "Maybe they'll come for us in a helicopter!"

"Do they have a helicopter at the lodge?" Jennifer didn't know whether she should let the younger girl comfort herself with fantasies that couldn't come true. She had started out trying to treat Darla as a contemporary, but perhaps it was kinder in the long run to let her build up her false hopes. She realized that it was harder than she had thought to know the right way to bring up a younger sister.

"There isn't any helicopter right at the lodge," said Darla. "But they could send for one. Of course, that would take time, too." The brightness was fading from her voice. "Trav's been gone an awful long time already."

Jennifer looked up at the moon again. It was moving across the night sky, but ever so slowly.

"I suppose you think this is all my fault," said Darla.

Jennifer didn't want to say yes, and she didn't want to lie. "It doesn't matter what I think," she said, finally.

"Yes, it does! And you *do* blame me. Everyone will!"

Not Travis, thought Jennifer. But she said, "The important thing is what *you* think."

"It was such beautiful snow," Darla said plaintively. "Too beautiful to resist."

Was it beautiful enough to trade a finger or a toe for? Jennifer wondered silently. Numbness was already creeping into her hands and feet. And Darla would be in worse shape, because she had been exposed for so much longer.

Darla sighed softly. "I'm sorry," she said. "It's all my fault, and I'm sorry."

"It will be all right," Jennifer said automatically. What else *could* she say?

"You're worried that something could have happened to Trav, aren't you?"

"He's safe by now. If he ran into any trouble, we would have heard the avalanche noise." She had to make herself believe that was true, or this night would be too terrible to bear.

"He'll be skiing all out," persisted Darla. "In the moonlight it's not so bad—but when he gets into the trees . . . He could break a leg, and that would be my fault, too."

Jennifer gave her a little shake. "Your brother is not going to break his leg. Don't even think such things. And yes, this *is* your fault, and I just hope you learn your lesson and never do such a reckless thing again."

"I'm sorry," Darla repeated, apparently somehow comforted at having brought on some of the scolding that she knew she deserved.

They lapsed into silence as time inched by and the moon slowly crossed over to the far rim of the canyon. Drowsiness stole up on them. Jennifer's head nodded. She jerked herself awake repeatedly, feeling that they shouldn't go to sleep in the snow. But they were both sound asleep with their arms around each other when the rescue party found them.

Jennifer opened her eyes to the sight of Travis's face. His hands were the ones that lifted her. But before she could grasp the reality of his presence, before she could reach out to him, other bodies came between them, other hands took her and wrapped her in warm blankets, fastened her securely to the rescue sled and started her on her way to the lodge, to the hospital. Before she was out of earshot, she had heard enough to know that Darla was not as fortunate as herself. The longer exposure had taken its toll, and the younger girl was only semiconscious.

Chapter Twenty

Jennifer tried to tell the doctors at the emergency room that she was all right, but the hospital personnel put her through a full battery of tests regardless, and acted in general as though they knew more about her condition than she did. They told her she was exhausted and put her firmly to bed. Then they immobilized her with an IV tube in her right arm. She couldn't get any information about Darla. And Travis did not come to see her.

He would be with Darla, of course. Darla was injured and suffering from exposure. Darla was his sister, his responsibility, the forlorn little waif who waved goodbye to him from the boarding school steps. And Jennifer had heartlessly threatened to leave that pathetic little bundle to wait alone in the snow—all to force the protective brother to take back his wretched parka. To give himself an equal chance to live.

At least he was *alive*. Lying alone in her expensive private room, she told herself to be satisfied with that. To stop watching the door so hopefully. Not to hold her breath each time footsteps sounded in the hall. The time of parting had been inevitably marching toward them all along. It had just arrived more quickly—more cruelly—than she had anticipated. Still, she watched the door. When her heavy eyelids could no longer hold back the pressing sleep, she let go and acknowledged that he would not come. It was over.

When she awoke she found herself curled into a tight ball. For a moment it was like being back in the snow cave—then she realized that she was warm. She stretched out luxuriously and turned toward the window. Mount Hood reared up ghostly white against the still grayness of early dawn, its volcanic peak looking as unadorned and symmetrical as a mountain drawn by a child. Behind it, the morning sky was just beginning to flush with rosy pink as the sun came up on a new day.

Jennifer's first thought was of Travis. She immediately set it aside. Be practical, she told herself. Think of food, of clothes. Of getting out of here. Of Darla. The first thing she must do was to find out if Darla was all right. After that, she would just leave this place. Very quietly. No tears, no recriminations.

The IV tube had vanished during the night, leaving a strip of bandage and tape on her arm. Jennifer reached for the button to summon a nurse. Then she reconsidered, remembering last night. One push would set in motion all the bossy busyness of hospital morning routine. She didn't need more doctors telling her what to do. There was no medicine here for the soreness in her heart. That was something only distance and time would heal.

With sudden resolution, she sat up and swung her legs over the side of the bed. And realized that the standard open-up-the-back hospital nightgown might keep her prisoner here more effectively than any doctor's orders could do. She hoped fiercely that yesterday's borrowed clothes would be hanging in the room's narrow closet.

There was an unexpected pair of feathery blue slippers on the floor at her bedside. She wondered a little as she slid her feet into the frivolous things. Some nurse's contribution? Surely not regular hospital equipment.

The closet held only a silky velour robe in a blue that matched the slippers—not as useful as her clothes would have been but better than nothing. She belted it around her purposefully. First she would find out about Darla. Then she would get on the telephone.

She opened the door cautiously, made sure no one was in the hallway and slipped out. She hesitated, looked around, wondering how she could avoid hospital personnel and still discover where they were keeping Darla.

The solution turned out to be as simple as glancing in at the open door of the room next to her own. The curly blond head on the pillow was unmistakable.

Jennifer shut the door behind her quietly. Darla raised her head at the click. Her face was streaked with tears.

Jennifer's heart went out to the girl. She came forward quickly. "What is it? Your knee? It's not frostbite—your fingers, your toes?"

Darla shook her head mutely. She wiped away fresh tears with her fingers. "It's Travis."

Jennifer felt the world slide out from under her. She clutched at the end of the bed for support. "What—what happened?"

"It's awful." Darla's voice rose in a wail and she went into a paroxysm of sobbing.

But Travis had to be all right, Jennifer told herself. He had been there to rescue them last night. He had lifted her in his arms. She'd seen his face. She hadn't been delirious or hallucinating. Had he survived the mountain only to meet with some other accident? Jennifer thought of the helicopter. She grasped Darla's arm, not gently. "Tell me," she commanded.

"I—I think he's got a concussion or something."

The world righted itself. At least he wasn't dead. "Go on."

"He's so strange. He's not like himself at all."

Jennifer's fingers relaxed their grip on Darla's arm. "Exactly what did he do?"

"Well—" Darla sniffled. "He's mad at me."

Jennifer gave her a severe look. "Don't you think he's entitled to be?"

"But I'm all right. *Everybody's* all right. He doesn't have to take it out on my car."

"Your *car*?"

"He says my darling little red Porsche is going straight back to the dealer." She turned wide eyes on Jennifer. "What has my sweet little car got to do with anything?"

"Didn't he explain at all?" asked Jennifer quietly.

"He did say something about not acting responsibly, and maybe I shouldn't even *have* a car if I can't be more careful. But I knew he couldn't really mean it. I asked him how I would manage when he goes away all the time if I was stuck without even a car to drive?—so he had to give in on that.''

For a moment Jennifer had felt a little spark of hope. If Travis had changed, had looked on his little sister with new eyes—but she should have known better than to hope. Of course he would give in, she thought drearily. ''So why all the tears?'' she said.

''He says that if—*if*—I get another car, then it will be a sedan. And it will be *gray*!''

''What's so terrible about that?''

Darla stared at her. ''But I don't *want* any old gray sedan. I want a sports car. A little red sports car.''

''Then why don't you earn one?'' said Jennifer.

Darla was speechless for a second. ''Me? I can't make my own money! I'm not a model or anything.''

''I mean—why don't you show Travis that you deserve one? You've been reckless and silly and caused an enormous amount of trouble. But you're a little old to spank. So why don't you take your medicine like a big girl? If you do get a stodgy sedan, then drive it without making a fuss. Drive it carefully, don't go too fast, don't get any tickets or wind up in any ditches. After a while, Travis will think you're entitled to trade up to a little younger style, a little prettier color—''

''And eventually I'll get my red sports car back!'' Darla finished excitedly, a smile chasing her tears.

Jennifer nodded, a little ruefully. "Or it's even possible you'll find that the thing you had your heart set on...might turn out to be not what you wanted after all."

These last words only brought a puzzled look to Darla's face, and Jennifer realized that she wasn't ready to hear them yet. That would take a few more years.... Jennifer turned to leave.

"Not that I'll be doing any driving for a week or two," said Darla. "Or skiing, either. I think I'll go back to the San Francisco house and let Mrs. Reilly fuss over me. Maybe you'd like to come along," she added. "I always have lots of fun in San Francisco."

Jennifer paused with her hand on the doorknob. She shook her head. "I'm afraid not, Darla. Goodbye."

The note of farewell in her voice apparently didn't penetrate Darla's consciousness. "You know, Jennifer, I'm really glad we had this talk," she said. "You'll see, I'm going to be good. Or at least I'll try."

Jennifer slipped back into her own room without being seen. Closing the door carefully, she turned to find Travis standing beside her empty bed. Vivid relief brightened his haggard face at the sight of her, telling her more than all the words she had longed to hear. Seeing him like this, with the grimness and anger wiped away, was like having the sun come up all over again.

He said, "By the time I got to your room last night, you were asleep." He opened his arms and she went to them like a homing dove. "And just now it looked as though I was too late again. I was afraid you'd left for good. Gone to Texas."

Her body was so filled with happiness that it seemed there was no room for breath. "I'm still here," she said, feeling light-headed.

"But will you stay?"

Her fingers touched his face, smoothing the lines of tiredness that were the evidence of his sleepless night. "If only I could," she said, with all the longing of her heart in her voice.

He looked down at her. "Are we going to start that again? This absolute obsession that you can't even trust your own emotions. And all because you once had a schoolgirl crush on Claude."

She stiffened. "You guessed?"

"Who else could it be?" he said. "You were seventeen years old; he was handsome and thirty and French. I'd say it was inevitable."

"You don't mind? And you don't hold it against Claude?"

He pulled her closer in a strong, comforting embrace. "I might say that it shakes my confidence in his judgment that he ever let you get away from him. But no, I don't hold it against him that you once thought you were in love with him. Because I've watched the two of you together, and it's plain that you're completely over it.''

Jennifer's heart sank. "But that's the whole problem," she said despairingly. "How can we know that it isn't going to happen again—"

Travis put a finger on her lips to silence her. "Because you're not a schoolgirl any more. You're a beautiful passionate woman." He kissed her with a fierce demanding fire.

When she could breathe again, she sighed deeply. "If only I could believe that.... I'd give anything to believe it...."

"If I could prove it to you, would you listen to me? Would you listen to Perry Mason for the defense one more time?"

She smiled sadly. "Even Perry needed some kind of evidence. There's no way you could know—"

"I know the things you've told me. It's all there, if you'll listen...."

She nodded. She would listen to anything, to any kind of nonsense if it meant she could stay in his arms just a few minutes longer.

He paused to organize his thoughts. "All right, here it is: you were seventeen—"

"Almost eighteen," she murmured defensively, her head resting against his chest.

"And in the throes of a very romantic and powerful infatuation, when the cruel tragedy of your father's heart attack tore you apart and drove you thousands of miles away from your beloved.''

"Don't make fun of me," she said.

"I don't mean to. But that's certainly the way you must have felt at the time. And when Claude wasn't present anymore, the infatuation never got to wear itself out in the usual manner. You were left with this fantasy lover you never got over. Perhaps you had dreams of someday coming back to Claude as a famous model, rich and sought after.''

Jennifer made a restless movement, and Travis knew that his shot in the dark had come close.

"But somewhere along the way you grew up. Modeling was an adolescent's kind of dream life as far as you were concerned. And your feelings for the handsome ski instructor—that was a teenager's kind of love dream. You got over one—and you got over the other. You grew up, Jennifer.''

"But I was so sure. I knew I loved him so much— that I would always love him. And I was wrong.''

"You're *entitled* to be wrong when you're almost eighteen. Would you trust Darla's judgment in affairs of the heart?'' He paused, but she remained silent. "No, you'd tell her to wait a while and see. Can't you just wait a while with me?''

"You really want me to stay?'' she murmured.

The strong arms tightened around her. "You know you never need to ask me that.''

"I think that I *should* ask from now on. No more jumping to conclusions. Every time I have tried to guess at your reactions, I've come up with the wrong answer. I don't really know you at all." His unshaven cheek brushed against hers.

"You know me better than anyone else. You know enough."

"I'm afraid that I don't," Jennifer said slowly. "Not yet."

He groaned. "Does that mean we have to wait all those years and years that you talked about, before you feel sure enough to marry me?"

"I'm sure about the way I feel," she said, knowing it was true. "I love you. I just think it would be nice if we could...get acquainted."

Travis drew back and frowned down at her, puzzled. "What do you mean? Formal introductions? Small talk?"

Shyness suddenly made her voice small. "I...I was just thinking...something more along the lines of—of a courtship," she said.

"A courtship," he said thoughtfully. "Not a long-distance one? With you in Fort Worth? Or Timbuktu?"

"No, nothing like that." It was hard for her to put it into words. "Just something...quiet."

"Oh, my dear." He drew her closer. "I don't know if what we have between us will ever be what you can call quiet. But let's give it a try. What shall it be—dinner dates and flowers?''

"And tennis matches and picnics and long walks in the moonlight." Her voice grew dreamy at the prospect.

"And you will tell me your life story. And listen to mine," he said, with the bantering note in his voice that Jennifer loved.

"I want you to meet my mother," she said.

"I'd love to meet your mother." Now his voice was serious, and she loved that, too.

She said, "I can't believe that when this morning came I was all ready to leave this place and go as far away as I could possibly go."

Travis stroked the silky sleeve of her robe caressingly. "That's why I only let them hang this in your closet. The rest of the clothes I ordered sent up are waiting at the nurses' station for you."

A wave of pure happiness made her a little giddy. "Plan Ahead MacKay," she said, gazing up into his face.

"That's me. All the time. But there *is* one problem," he added, more seriously.

At any other time in their relationship, those words would have struck terror into her heart. Now she knew that a problem meant something that the two of them would work out together.

"One day soon I'm going to have to get on a plane to Kansas City," he went on.

In the excitement of the moment, she had forgotten about that. "I guess I'll have to come down to the plane and wave goodbye to you." She tried not to sound disappointed.

"The last thing I ever want to do is to say goodbye to you again. Come with me, Jennifer. Bring your cameras along."

She had to smile. "To Kansas City?"

"I'm sure a really good photographer could do wonders with Kansas City." Travis kissed her lightly and held her closer.

"Perhaps you're right," she said after a moment.

"And something tells me it would be a wonderful place to start a honeymoon."

All of a sudden she was breathless. "What about our courtship?"

"Is there a law it has to come *before* the wedding? I'm sure Kansas City has flowers and moonlight." He saw the sudden trepidation in her eyes and relented. "All right, courtship first, honeymoon later. Everything just the way you want it. Just as long as you're *with* me. We can have separate rooms—separate *hotels*—whatever you say. And I'll go off to work in the daytime, and we'll dance and romance every night...."

She nestled closer into his arms. "You're always so busy. Are you sure that's what you want? Me trailing along behind you—?"

His embrace tightened. "*Beside* me. Always beside me. You can be immortalizing Kansas City on film. Or Singapore. Wherever we are. As long as we're together. I thought I loved this business—the wheeling and dealing—more than anything on earth. Now I only know that if I have to leave you behind, I don't want to go. And I never met any woman who could make me feel that way before. I don't dare let you out of my sight, you're apt to disappear, like fairy gold. And the day—the *minute*—that you feel our courtship is complete, you'll tell me. And the honeymoon can begin." He paused. "Don't make it *too* long, will you?"

She smiled against his chest. Separate rooms, indeed! When every sight of him, every touch only made the magic stronger, made her desire him more. The long careful months she had envisioned began to shrink in her mind, collapse in upon themselves. Maybe in the spring, she thought. The very early spring.

He looked down at her expectantly, and she knew this was the moment of truth. Did she dare to follow her heart, to give him the answer he was waiting for?

"It won't be long at all," she said.

His eyes lit up with a great joy. He claimed her lips with a fierce possessiveness. As her body kindled in response to his, Jennifer let herself realize that all the things he had told her were true. In his arms she had become a woman. This, at last, was love.

* * * * *

Silhouette Special Edition

COMING NEXT MONTH

#421 NO ROOM FOR DOUBT—Tracy Sinclair
No job too small or too difficult, Stacey Marlowe's ad boasted. But then she hadn't considered the demands her first customer would make. Shady Sean Garrison wanted—of all things!—her trust.

#422 INTREPID HEART—Anne Lacey
Trent Davidson would forever be a hero to Vanessa Hamilton. After all, he'd twice saved her life. But how could Trent settle for Vanessa's childlike adoration when he needed her womanly love?

#423 HIGH BID—Carole Halston
Katie Gamble was thrilled when fellow building contractor Louis McIntyre reentered her life. But Louis's gentle deception—and uneasy memories of a night long ago—threatened their bid for a future together.

#424 LOVE LYRICS—Mary Curtis
Ambitious lyricist Ashley Grainger lived and breathed Broadway, while her former fiancé, conservative lawyer Zachary Jordan, was Boston born and bred. Despite their renewed duet of passion, could they possibly find a lasting harmony?

#425 SAFE HARBOR—Sherryl Woods
When sexy neighbor Drew Landry filed a complaint about Tina Harrington's unorthodox household, they battled it out in the boardroom . . . and the bedroom . . . even as they longed for sweet compromise.

#426 LAST CHANCE CAFE—Curtiss Ann Matlock
Rancher Wade Wolcott wanted no part of Ellie McGrew's struggle to build a new life for her daughters. But the lovely, unassuming widow bought the farm next door, waited tables in his diner—and somehow crept into his heart.

AVAILABLE THIS MONTH:

#415 TIME AFTER TIME
Billie Green

#416 FOOLS RUSH IN
Ginna Gray

#417 WHITE NIGHTS
Dee Norman

#418 TORN ASUNDER
Celeste Hamilton

#419 SUMMER RAIN
Lisa Jackson

#420 LESSONS IN LOVING
Bay Matthews